GOOD BOY

BOOKS BY CLAIRE DEAN

✦

GIRLWOOD

SPIRIT CALLER

BOOKS BY CHRISTY YORKE

✦

THE WISHING GARDEN

MAGIC SPELLS

SONG OF THE SEALS

SUMMER OF GLORIOUS MADNESS

THE SECRET LIVES OF THE SUSHI CLUB

Long Creek Books edition 2020

Copyright @ 2020 by Claire Dean

ISBN 978-0-9986025-3-0

1. Pets 2. Fiction General

Printed in the United States of America

For Sugar, Sam, Cleo, Luna, Jenny, Nike, and all the good dogs.

1

The woman who fills his water bowl sweats magnificently and, even better, she fails to latch the door. One leap to lick the salty beads from her neck, then he bursts from his cell, charging down the row of black mutts and last-chance pit bulls who bark jealously at his escape. Turning the corner too quickly, he skids across the concrete, then snaps at one of the celebrity terriers who never stay long. As the woman runs after him, he dodges and feints, evading her easily. For a big dog, he's amazingly nimble, but his real specialty is speed. He's fled through the back exit twice, where it took half a dozen shelter workers to corner him in the gated, pee-soaked yard, so this time he chases a couple carrying two rodent-sized chihuahuas in their arms. He's a black blur as they leap out of the way, but behind them stands the two men who bathe him. He turns on a dime, but one of them grabs his collar while the other pokes him in the hip.

When he wakes, he's returned to his cell. He shakes off the grogginess by pacing, ten feet to one padlock, then ten to the other. When the toy dogs yap at a new visitor, he flings himself against the chain link. People come all the time, smelling of excitement and pity and other places, but they always stop before reaching him, the moment any dog under ten pounds wags her tail. He doesn't even bother to bark a greeting before running in circles. He likes to see how fast he can spin and is nearing top speed when the woman who fills his water bowl brings a stranger down his row.

The new man smells antiseptically clean, almost not worth sniffing, but on the other hand he stops to watch him spin.

". . . black ones are the hardest to adopt out," the woman is saying. " . . . not really sure. . . black Lab, part Great Dane, all jerk." She laughs, but the man doesn't. "Gotta get the special leash for him . . . escape artist."

He is dizzy now, so he sits to chew his tail while the man crouches, pressing his large hands against the metal links of the cell. He is as thin and colorless as a greyhound—pallid skin, pale hair, dust-colored clothing. The people who get this close are usually yelling, but when the man speaks, his voice is soft and gravelly, lightly used.

"Good boy," he says. "That's a good boy."

He could growl, but the woman is opening his cell door. This time, she blocks the exit with her body as she clips the double-wide, steel leash to his collar. Then suddenly the man called Good Boy is double-looping the leash around his wrist and leading him outside.

The small yard is crammed with people petting excited terriers, so he barks and lunges until most of them leap away. With a grunt, Good Boy yanks him toward the fence. There is nowhere to go except in circles, first at a walk, then a trot, then with a quick sideways glance at the man, a sprint. Surprisingly, there is no tug on the leash as Good Boy keeps up with him. His jowls flap and the wind smells like freedom, even if it isn't. They run until he's panting and he hears the man's heart racing, and the woman who fills his water bowl approaches to ask, "Had enough of him yet?"

He presses his flank against Good Boy's thigh as the man leans forward, chest heaving. The stench of soap has been obliterated by tangy sweat and something vinegary. Good Boy stares down at him as the woman reaches for the leash.

"Actually," Good Boy says, "I think I'm going to keep him."

The woman steps back abruptly and shouts at the man by the door. "You hear that, Mike? He's taking the monster!" Then she throws her hands in the air and shouts, "We're free!"

Anything is better than his cell, but in Good Boy's house bleach coats everything that might have once been worth inhaling; one lick of the wooden tabletop and his tongue burns. There isn't a crumb or pee stain to be found, not even under the beds. He pads into two dark, empty rooms, whacks his tail harmlessly at tables devoid of knickknacks. Nose to the floor, he finally finds a hint of stale perfume in the corner of the bathroom, but much more interesting is the large bedroom next to it, and the fluffy, brown comforter on the bed.

He springs atop the mattress, digging out a soft spot in the blanket before Good Boy finds him and yells, "Off!" He understands a few words, and "Off" is one he doesn't care for. People say it too much, pushing him away from their most alluring body parts, dragging him off countertops to ground level. They want him smaller when actually, if he hoists his forepaws onto the headboard, his head almost touches the ceiling!

Good Boy yells "Off!" again, but like most words it's ignorable, particularly once he dodges Good Boy's grasp. The man gets little more than a fingernail on his fur before he's down the hall and into a room with another bed that isn't nearly as soft to jump on, then on to the kitchen. He slows down to make it interesting, feinting left then hurtling right. Good Boy stops chasing him long enough to lean against the counter, then opens a cupboard and pours kibble into a bowl.

He turns his nose away from the smell of familiar cellblock rations and snatches a much more appealing plastic water bottle from the counter. Happily, this turns out to be the very same toy that Good Boy wants! They play tug of war, sliding across the kitchen floor, knocking over the bowl of kibble before he wins and runs away with his prize. In the bathroom, he drops the bottle to sniff a white toilet bowl with the best scents in the whole house. He laps up the water until Good Boy pushes him off and closes the lid. With no more rooms to explore, he allows Good Boy to maneuver him back to the kitchen. Then, in an act that seals their friendship forever, the man opens a can of meaty goo and spills it into the bowl.

Even counting the bones and trash he once scavenged, and the basted rawhide they used to lure him out of the woods, nothing has ever tasted so good. He licks the bowl clean, then follows Good Boy to the kitchen table, where the man sits and puts his head in his hands.

Without the constant barking and rattling of chain link, he hears other things—a ticking sound, flies ramming themselves against the window pane, Good Boy swallowing as he rubs his thumb across his wrist. The man still reeks of soap but his knee is the perfect height for a tall dog's chin. When Good Boy pats his head awkwardly, he doesn't move. He is as still as he has ever been.

"I'm going to name you Toby," Good Boy says. "Okay, Toby?"

He wags his tail at the soft voice, leans against the man to soak up his heat.

"You want to go outside, Toby?"

Good Boy stands and leads him into the backyard, where there are two large trees and garden beds he'd dig up if it weren't for Good Boy presenting him with a furry hedgehog that squeaks every time he tries to tear it in half. He thrashes the toy with his teeth, flings it sideways and chases after it, then runs happily in circles. The entire yard is a delight—soft grass, the scent of voles underfoot, white moths to snap at as he runs. He flushes two doves from a bush and sprints along the fence line, where an old woman sits atop the cedar planks and laughs when he jumps right through her legs. He can see the last rays of the sun through her arms; she hums a tune that makes him stop and cock his head. Her scent is intoxicating, as if every place she's been and everything she's ever tasted, touched, and kissed is stored inside her and oozing out through her pores. He licks her gossamer toes and breathes her in until Good Boy says, "Toby, come!"

People like to call him something, and he doesn't mind Toby. It's possible he might even answer to it at some point.

Later, after Good Boy has removed him twice from the big bed and laid delicious biscuits all around the carpet for him to find, he listens to the sounds within the silence of his new home—the rustling of the sheets as Good Boy turns over, the old woman still humming from the fence, a distant cat's mewl. Thankfully, he is wide awake when Good Boy cries out in his sleep, so it is no effort at all to return to the big bed and curl up beside him. As Good Boy quiets, his eyelids get heavy and he sighs deeply. It will be the best sleep of his life.

2

His favorite things:

Tennis balls.
Doorbells.
Any food from a can.
Getting a treat without having to do anything.
The sound of Good Boy's key in the lock.
Things that rip.
Newly turned dirt.

Toilet bowls.

Whatever Good Boy's eating.

The way Good Boy calls him Toby and strings their names together into one thing— "GoodBoyTobyGoodBoy."

People who don't push him down when he jumps on them.

Everything out the front door.

The men down the street who call him "Perro gigantico" and let him drink from their thermoses.

Barking choruses.

The sight of Good Boy holding the leash.

Being the biggest.

The smell of everything.

Good Boy's bed.

Any body of water.

Anything that runs.

Any day that begins and ends with Good Boy.

Even soap.

Things he dislikes:

Terriers.

The ginger cat who trespasses in his yard.

The man who comes to walk him when Good Boy is gone.

The nights when Good Boy won't wake even when he licks him.

The mornings when Good Boy cries.

Toby's entire backside wags when the girl walks in. She's dressed in colors
he can see, neon yellow on top, turquoise blue on the bottom, and she
saturates the room with a smorgasbord of fragrance—cut grass and soda
pop, bubblegum and cigarettes, vomit, disinfectant, talcum powder, clove.
He presses his nose into her stomach and salivates, licks her knee through
the hole in her jeans. Her dark curly hair falls around her smiling face; her
fingernails and shoes are gold. She's like the sun falling out of the sky.

She bends to pet him, and her voice is dazzling. From the moment
she enters the house, she talks incessantly, her words blending together into
one magnificent song.

"... noidea.   I'veappliedeverywhere. . . gasstationsthedinerby . . .
LOVEthechancetoworkwithadog!"

Toby leaps on her, draping his paws around her shoulders to lick the
luscious hollow of her neck.

"Toby, off!" Good Boy says. "Down!!!"

Good Boy wrenches him off her as she goes right on talking. In just
a few seconds, she utters more words than Good Boy has spoken the entire
time Toby has known him.

"... That's so . . . hadacollie . . . momgotacatbutsheneverreally . . .
LOVE dogs!" she says.

Good Boy gestures toward the sofa that, until yesterday, had a
shaggy rug beneath it.   When Toby woke, he searched for it for hours,

hoping to tear out the rest of the wool pile. The girl sits, still talking, and Toby makes a U-turn, nestling his rump into the pillow of her thighs.

". . . no replies to my ad," Good Boy says. "It's Sylvia, right? I was worried . . . maybe word had gotten out about Toby."

Toby's ears perk up at the name he usually responds to, unless he's gotten off leash, or is squirrel-stalking, or the ginger cat is in the yard. He likes the name, unless Good Boy screams it. Of all the words he knows, most are nonsense and the rest untrustworthy. "Sit" lands him treats, but also stops him from leaping at the mailman. "Don't eat that!" steals the manure right out of his mouth. "Come" leads to praise or punishment, "walk" is the start of a great adventure, but often ends in misery, when he's dragged away from a new neighbor or the upstart golden Lab. There are a lot of words designed to get him to do things, but less for what he wants to do. And to be honest, aside from Good Boy, he prefers women's voices, the higher the better, accompanied by bare legs slathered in lotion and fingers in his ears. Everything he needs to know can be conveyed with the touch of a hand.

" . . . rescue, so they don't know," Good Boy is saying. "They found him in the woods somewhere . . . just me here. I thought . . . totally different than what I imagined . . . good dog but a bit defiant."

Good Boy runs a hand through his dust-colored hair, the way he does whenever Toby proudly shows off a sock he's chewed or the remains of the lilac bush. Toby moves just enough to lick the girl's ankles. She tastes even better than she smells, of coconut-flavored lotion and tangy perspiration. She doesn't push his head away, but merely scratches his backside with her long, divine fingernails.

" . . . had a dog," she says. Her voice drifts in and out of his awareness as Toby feasts on her legs. " . . . cleanedandwalkedhim . . . liketotallyadogperson."

The only other person who sat in their living room was the man who used to walk Toby every morning, after he put a spiked metal collar around his neck. Whenever Toby lunged at a chipmunk, the metal tines stabbed him, so one day, when the man bent to retie his shoe, Toby bolted so suddenly he snapped the leash and avoided capture until dusk. When the man dragged him home and slammed a boot into his ribs, Good Boy flew out the front door, speaking in a growl Toby had never heard before.

"Don't. Ever. Touch. My. Dog. Again."

Half a dozen words. No nonsense.

When the girl finally pauses for breath, Good Boy clears his throat. "I need someone to spend time with him," he says. "Walk him or . . . just don't let him destroy everything. The pay is twelve an hour."

"Oh my God, I would LOVE to make that!" the girl says immediately. "IwouldLOVEit! ThisissoamazingI . . ."

She talks faster and faster, until the only word he can make out is LOVE. Toby swishes his tail as he watches her mouth move. LOVE reminds him of the magpies that squawk just to hear themselves. He can sit outside and watch them all day.

"You don't have school?" Good Boy cuts in.

"Um, yeahsoit'skindofalongstory?" Her voice rises every few seconds when she comes up for air. "I LOVED school, but then. . . mom'scancer . . . hadtohelpathome . . . justherandme."

She actually goes quiet then, which allows Toby to hear the racing of her heart. A sniffle here, nervous gulp there, a bird (maybe a magpie!) flying past the window.

"I don't mean to pry," Good Boy says. "I just need someone dependable. Toby can be strong-willed . . . weighs more than you do."

LOVE smiles and scratches Toby behind his ears. Her eyes are the same color as the earth when he digs up the flower beds.

"Oh, I can handle him," she says. "I'mstrongerthanIlook! Toby's a LOVE, I can just tell."

Another favorite thing: LOVE.

She doesn't bring a choke collar or yell at him when he jumps. Instead of hitting him after he escapes her, she laughs and says, "Slippery fish." They walk every day, and she rarely yanks him away from whatever he's sniffing. When she heads one way and he goes another, she usually follows his tug, sometimes singing, sometimes taking out her phone to say, ". . . el monstruo, mamá. Estaré en casa pronto."

They walk everywhere! Past urine-stained lawns and deliciously sweaty men jogging by with music leaking from their ears, stalking silently toward robins until they fly away in terror. Today, he trots through a cloud of white moths, swallowing three before they scatter. Toby's nose twitches left and right, finding lemons, gasoline, sewer gas, spilled wine. There is bird poop on the sidewalk, a splash of coffee on the curb. And the ginger cat has been here. He tracks her scent past four houses, then comes to a halt at the pungent marker of a male dog. The dog's been neutered and would challenge even Toby for domination. Probably that golden Labrador that is always passing by the front window, flaunting the fact that he's off leash. Toby raises a leg to pee over the mark, then back-kicks the scent for good measure.

LOVE tugs at him and begins talking again, in that rapid-fire way that sounds more like bird calls than words.

"Ohmygodyoumustbeliketwohundredpounds!"

She tries to pull him onward, but there's a fly buzzing past his ear.

" . . . moveyourgiant . . . perro loco . . ."

He spots the ginger cat's tail disappearing behind a bush and leans forward, tailed raised, every muscle in his body taut. The fly lands on his ear and he ignores it. Even LOVE disappears. He stares intently at the bush and lifts his right front paw slightly, waiting for the cat's next move. When he finally spots the flick of a tail, he springs.

He barely notices the weight he drags along with him, or the screaming in his ear. The cat darts from bush to driveway to the underside of a boxy brown car. Toby slides to a stop, unable to stuff more than his head beneath the bumper, two feet from the hissing cat. He barks madly, scrambling from one side of the car to the other. The cat's scent is everywhere—on the concrete, the hood of the car, the path to the small white house—more pervasive and unendurable than soap. He leans sideways, swiping at golden eyes until he is suddenly yanked back. LOVE has wrapped the leash around her wrist and is on the ground dragging him, allowing the ginger cat to escape to a nearby tree. The beast scampers up the trunk and out along a limb too high for Toby to reach, then turns and fixes him with her steady, yellow gaze. Sounds return—the fly again, a car driving past, LOVE breathing hard and getting to her feet, scolding him.

"Bad dog!"

Toby pants happily. That was the closest he's ever gotten to the cat! He steps toward the tree, ready for round two, before LOVE brushes off her backside and snaps his lead. She tugs him toward the sidewalk, but manages only one step before the door to the white house opens and the woman from the fence steps out.

Clinging to the porch railing, she walks down the steps with difficulty, wearing only one shoe. She no longer hums, saying "Lola, lola, lola" instead, as tears stream down her cheeks.

"Ma'am?" LOVE says, leading Toby up the walk. "Are you all right?"

"Lola?"

LOVE takes the woman's arm as a white-haired man hobbles out the front door. Toby recognizes him as the man in the house behind Good Boy's, the one who likes to spray him with the hose when he barks. Toby always opens his mouth to catch the water and sometimes barks for no reason, just to start the game. Plus, it makes the woman on the fence laugh.

She doesn't laugh now. The man removes LOVE's hand and replaces it with his own, but the old woman doesn't look at him.

"Phyllis," he says, "come back now. I've got your program on."

"Lola, lola, lola," she replies.

"Let's go back inside."

The woman on the fence always smiles, but this woman cries without sound. And no matter how feverishly Toby sniffs her, he can't smell anything. Certainly no lifetime of aromas; not even a whiff of perfume or sweat. He's not entirely convinced she's real.

"Do you need some help?" LOVE asks the man with the hose.

He grips Lola's arm tighter and turns to glare. "No, I do not need your help, young woman. What I need is for you to get your monster dog off my lawn."

"Today," LOVE says a few days later, "is totally tragic."

Toby wags his tail. He's smelled six dogs, licked a wad of discarded bubblegum, and eaten the remains of an oily napkin and a red plastic cup! The squirrels have been especially exuberant, making death-defying leaps from tree to tree. Toby runs to a towering elm and leaps at the boldest one, chee-cheeing from a daringly low branch.

"OhmyGodwouldyougiveitarest!"

LOVE tugs him forward, but he's a master at resistance. It takes all of LOVE's strength to drag him to the corner, and the truth is he wouldn't have moved at all if it weren't for the smell of blood. Toby's nose twitches as he makes out a few specifics—male dog, unneutered, the wound a day or two old. Toby spots the dog tied to a tree in front of a ramshackle house— stocky and barrel-chested, with a sand-colored body and wide, mottled face. Neither of them bark immediately. Toby turns his ears forward; the other dog stretches his tail horizontally and waits. The blood is caked on the dog's neck where the rope has chafed his fur away; his water bowl is empty. When he opens his mouth, it is not to curl his lips, but to pant.

The tension drains from Toby's body. The dog approaches him hesitantly, head down the way Toby likes it, but comes up short at the end of his rope. By the time he flicks his tail playfully, Toby is already halfway across the yard. There is a satisfying snap when the leash pops out of LOVE's hand.

"Toby!"

He ignores LOVE's cries and the dead lawn's treasure trove of cigarette butts and beer cans to circle the dog. He's not a fan of his smell—blood mixed with smoke and too much grass for breakfast—but at least the mutt cowers when Toby sniffs him.

Then they run. Or, rather, Toby flaunts his speed while the dog yelps each time he comes up short at the end of his tether. Toby play-bites the dog's neck; the dog throws a paw over Toby's shoulder and knocks him backwards. The dog is smaller than him but strong, and unlike the lazy Labradors at the dog park, he keeps running even after he's foaming at the mouth.

"TOBY!"

LOVE lunges for Toby's harness, so he makes a sudden left turn and sprints around the yard. He hurdles folding chairs and a rusted barbecue, plows through an old pile of ash, a half-burned stump and broken bottles. The other dog runs to one side of the tree then the other, barking and straining at the rope to catch him, and Toby circles even faster, the wind stinging his eyes, jowls flapping.

"OhmyGodcomehereyoustupidbeast!"

And then it's over. A shirtless man steps out of the house, startling Toby with his fiery scent, and LOVE dives for the leash. The man grabs one of the broken glass bottles from the ground and whacks it against the other dog's head.

"Shut the hell up!"

The dog whines as the man grabs his tether and forces him twice around the tree, until he's left with only two feet of freedom. Toby rarely fails to jump on new people, but that's because until now none of them have smelled like a burning building, like something you run away from instead of running toward. The man is shorter and thinner than Good Boy, with shoulder-length, dark hair hanging over even darker eyes. Even his fingertips are blackened; there are ashes in the dark hairs on his chest. He drops the bottle and the fur on Toby's neck bristles. He steps in front of LOVE as the man turns to stare.

"Oh," she says.

The dark man shows his teeth. "Better keep your dog leashed. I'm surprised this one didn't kill him."

"He seems sweet."

"He'll attack anything that moves. Named him Sunshine. For a joke. Right, Sunshine?"

The man gathers the rope around Sunshine's neck until the dog gasps for air and squirms to get away.

"Stop it!" LOVE says, stepping forward.

The dark man loosens the rope and shrugs. "He's just a dog."

"People who hurt dogs have bad luck," LOVE says.

The dark man brushes his hair from his eyes and looks her over from top to bottom, and in that moment Toby can't smell LOVE at all. Every last delicious scent is gobbled up by fire. The dark man laughs and walks back into the house, letting the door slam behind him. LOVE crosses the yard until she reaches Sunshine and pets him until he stops trembling, but when she stands again and looks at the house, it's her hand that shakes.

"Dios mío!" she says. "He is so hot."

3

There is no night or day, summer or winter; there is only being with the ones he loves. When Good Boy leaves the world ends, and Toby barks and chews the chair legs until it starts up again. He stares at the last place he saw the man; if no one comes, he panics and defecates by the door. He knows Good Boy will yell, but yelling requires a presence and a beating is still a touch. When the key turns in the lock, he pees in anticipation for life to start over.

All he wants in this world is to never be alone in it.

Tonight, when Good Boy opens the door, Toby sidesteps the pile of feces and throws his long forepaws around Good Boy's neck. He licks his face to decipher his absence—dirt and gasoline, a ketchup-slathered hamburger, salt, stress, sea air. He will stand on his hind legs as long as Good Boy will tolerate it. Good Boy smiles and hugs him until he sees the damage done.

"Oh, Toby," he says, and pushes Toby off. Toby tucks his tail between his legs and cowers in the corner as Good Boy cleans the mess. He makes himself as small as he can, a tiny good dog that will be either adored or overlooked. Good Boy takes the paper towels and cleaners back to the kitchen before returning to Toby's side. Toby rarely thinks about his life before Good Boy, but today he remembers the man who took him to the woods and drove off too fast for even him to catch. He leans closer to Good Boy, close enough to be struck or to follow, and trembles.

Good Boy crouches and holds Toby's chin in his hand.

"Dumb dog," he says softly, and Toby looks up. He licks Good Boy's cheek, Good Boy taps him lightly on the nose, and everything is right again. They play tug-of-war with the hedgehog for a few minutes before beginning Good Boy's favorite game.

Sometimes Good Boy paces for a while first; other times he can't wait to begin. Tonight, they pause together outside the bathroom door while Good Boy presses his fists to his eyes. Toby nudges the door open with his nose, then retreats proudly, tail wagging. Twice a day, Toby gets to drink from the gleaming white bowl while Good Boy glares at the other Good Boy in the mirror. The men size each other up like warring alpha dogs, nothing but hatred in their eyes. They both open a bottle and pour white, oval-shaped pills into their hands. Sometimes they draw out the moment by putting the pills back inside the bottle before taking them out again, but more often than not they simply swallow them quickly, then hunch over the sink. Tonight, Good Boy turns his back on the mirror and, when Toby finishes his drink and stares at him, says, "Shut up, Toby." Toby wags his tail.

He is with the one he loves and life is perfect.

LOVE struggles to put on his harness as Toby leaps and licks her arms. Everything out the door is good, but the taste of coconut lotion is better.

"ILOVEyoutooTobyohmygod!" LOVE says.

When she opens the door, he trades lotion for the scents brought in by last night's rain. Moldy leaves, rotting deck posts, jasmine. Skunk and humus and something long dead washed away into the sewer drain. He pauses on the top step, nose twitching, until LOVE tugs his harness and leads him not to the sidewalk, but to her car.

She opens the door and he sinks to the cement. For all his speed, he can also make himself part of the pavement. Before cars became a trap, he would stick his head out the window, inhaling everyone and everything. But now he knows where cars will take him—to forests or metal cages, to places the ones he loves can't find.

"It's just the car!" she says, yanking on his harness. He could growl, but she is the one who lets him up on the couch and gives him the remains of her sandwiches. It's just as simple to wait for her to tire.

"Dogs LOVE cars!"

He doesn't even have to claw at the concrete to resist her; she can't move him an inch. When she pauses for breath, he rolls onto his back. LOVE puts her hands on her hips, then crouches beside him.

"Come on now," she says, rubbing his belly.   He stretches out luxuriously. "That's my boy. That's a good boy."

At the sound of Good Boy's name, he glances at the car. When she stops rubbing him and pulls his leash again, he trembles as he stands. She doesn't force him, so he inches forward and sniffs the open door.   The interior smells like LOVE plus spilled soda, and even more enticing are the potato chip crumbs strewn across the front seat. He climbs in to reach them as LOVE laughs and closes the door.

When she rolls down the windows, he almost forgets where they might be headed. Every second brings a different scent—Doberman, grass suntan lotion, plastic, exhaust smoke, squirrel, coffee, grapefruit, death cigarettes, urine, sizzling meat.   He can't wait to smell the wonders on LOVE's side and crawls across her lap.

"MyGodTobyI'mdriving!" she shouts and shoves him back. He gets wedged with one paw on either side of the gear shift, and when she stops suddenly, he lurches painfully into the back seat. But there is a bit of old apple there that is tasty and tough to swallow, and when he sticks his head out one window then the other, his drool paints the side of the car.

The longer they drive, the more unfamiliar the scents—some kind of acrid smoke, spicy gray plants, parched earth. There are fewer cars to bark at while the landscape shrinks from skyscrapers to houses to barren brown hills. By the time the car finally slows, all he smells is dust. They pull up over hard-packed soil to a small, squat house.

The one he loved did not get out. He reached past Toby to fling open the door and used the steel heel of his boot to kick Toby out.

LOVE's shoes are made of rubber so soft Toby can break the heel in one bite, and when she steps out of the car, the first thing she grabs is Toby's leash. One tug is all he needs to jump into the front seat and out her door. When he leans against her, he realizes she is trembling too.

"I need you to behave, all right?" she says, sounding as slow and hoarse as Good Boy.

Toby's tail rises.   There are no trees to check for squirrels, no squawking birds or unfamiliar cars to attack. He strains to sniff something other than dirt and finds a distant scent of mourning dove, along with the trail of a cat who might have once prowled the yard but hasn't gone out for weeks.

At the front door, LOVE pauses, then goes in without knocking. Toby freezes with two paws in, two out. All the potted plants on the porch are dead. The house is stifling, even with the blinds closed to sunlight; the stale air reeks of vomit and dead skin and breath laced with rot. The house smells not of death, but of dying, and he whimpers.

"Hola mamá," LOVE says softly, tugging on Toby's leash.

The woman on the sofa only whispers.   Toby doesn't want to approach her, but he will follow wherever LOVE goes.   Every dog knows that dying is simple. When it's time, you dig a hole beneath a tree and lie in it.   The rest takes care of itself.   But there are no trees outside, and the woman is trapped in stale blankets, with only her thin white hair and cadaver-like face sticking out. It's all Toby can do to find an open stretch of neck to sniff.

LOVE nudges him away.   "Lo siento, mamá. Este es Toby. Es un maníaco."

The dying woman turns her gaze to Toby and, after a moment, one corner of her mouth slowly turns up. She wriggles her gnarled fingers out from under the blanket to touch the fur at his neck. Her skin is icy, which feels glorious in the sweltering room.

"Es magnífico," she says.

LOVE sits with her a while, saying nothing, then drops Toby's leash and walks into the back room. When she returns a few minutes later in a shiny dress and pointed shoes, Toby doesn't budge. The dying woman has fallen asleep with her hand on his neck. Her breathing is labored, but every once in a while she makes a sound like a sigh and her grip on him tightens.

LOVE removes the woman's hand and places it beneath the covers. Then she kisses her head and reclaims Toby's leash. They walk outside, where the cool autumn day is like a shock of life itself. LOVE is crying; Toby leans into her until she stumbles sideways in her funny shoes.

"ForGod'ssakeToby," she says, shoving him then pulling him back instantly. She holds him so tight it's hard to lick her ear, but he manages.

It is only as they drive away that he gets a glimpse of the back yard and what stands in the middle of it—a spindly, four-foot oak struggling for life in the unyielding earth. The only tree for miles. The perfect dying tree.

LOVE walks so slowly in her funny shoes that Toby is able to mark a dozen lampposts and twice as many mailboxes before they reach Sunshine's yard. The dog is still tied to the tree, his fur matted with burrs and dust, but he clambers to his paws and flicks his tail as they approach. Toby expects a tug as he trots across the dead grass, but instead LOVE loosens his lead and tries to keep up. She stares at the house and tucks her curly hair behind her ear, but it comes loose again almost instantly when her heel disappears in the grass. She grunts as she stumbles, but by then Toby has a paw around Sunshine's neck and is taking him to the ground.

Dust flies as they wrestle, Sunshine rolling on top of him, Toby happily gnawing at his neck.   Somewhere LOVE is yelling, but she must have given up on the leash because when Toby lands a kick to Sunshine's ribs and gains his footing, he's free.   He flies around the tree, nipping at Sunshine every time he passes, dazzling even himself with his speed.   A car whizzes past, but just as he starts racing it he spots the shadow perched in the scarlet-leafed tree across the street.

He comes to a sudden stop as what began as a trick of the light rises to the shape of a man.   The figure stands six feet tall and broad shouldered without breaking the slender branch beneath it, and Sunshine barks a warning.   The shadow flinches and creeps forward tentatively, as if, until that moment, it didn't realize it could be seen.

"Whatareyoulookingat?" LOVE asks, finally freeing her heel from the lawn.   She reaches for Toby's leash, but not before he takes off running just as the shadow drops noiselessly from the tree.   After that, there is only chaos, and a most unlikely pair of creatures reveling in being free.

4

"Toby, come!" LOVE yells.

Obviously, he ignores her.

He can outrun anyone, human or canine, but when he reaches the scarlet tree, the shadow is gone. Toby puts his nose to the ground, but the only trail he finds leads to gopher holes and the people who live in the big white house beside the tree. One paints her toenails, another smells like candy, the dog in the house is female, spayed, and fond of eating the landscape, which is a delicious mix of dandelions and clover. Toby nibbles at the bright green leaves as LOVE runs awkwardly toward him in her funny shoes.

"That's a good boy," she says, slowing her pace, holding her hands out in front of her as if she could grab him at any moment. He knows this game! He gets low and allows her to come within three feet, then two. "Just let me get y—"

Then he's off! LOVE dives for the leash trailing behind him, but he's lightning quick, untouchable. He leaps onto the porch, knocks over a gray vase of even grayer, brittle flowers, and launches himself off the other side. Kicking up clouds of dust and dandelion tufts, he flies around the corner, into an alley with dozens of delectably-scented blue garbage bins set out for pick-up. He hears LOVE's slow-motion footsteps behind him as he topples one of the cans and nabs the remains of a bean burrito, all without missing a step. The alley stretches for blocks and, once he's up to full speed, there's no way he'll stop. He's a black flash; it must look like he's flying.

"Tobyyyyyyyy!" LOVE calls from somewhere far behind him.

He lengthens his stride and bites at the wind. Love, he thinks. LOVE!

By the time Toby flops onto the warm pavement, his tongue lolls out the side of his mouth and the sky is the color of spoiled plums. He's seen so many marvels, he can hardly remember them all. Charcoal barbecues, curbs brimming with moldering leaves and pumpkin innards, even a concrete-lined river with the most delectable coating of green scum. He ran unchecked through fields and out where the scrub oak gives way to junipers, going as far as he wanted because one sniff of the air would always lead him home. Now he rolls onto his back, foam ringing his mouth, every part of him aching. He can't imagine how this day could get any better, until he smells the rats.

They scrabble through the walls of the dilapidated building behind him, their pungent odor making his nostrils twitch. He leaps to his feet and digs at the building's foundation, cocking his head every time the rats scramble off in fear. He's been known to dig for hours, but tonight he stops when a flock of black birds swoops from one tree to the next. Good Boy usually brings him inside before dark, so he's almost forgotten how loud the crickets can be. He lays down just to listen, their voices lulling him to sleep like the ticking of Good Boy's clock. He loves his dreams almost as much as he loves real life; he's never had a single one where he's alone. This time he's with LOVE and the dying woman, eating a cake of fluttering moths so delicious he has to lie down to eat it. He can still feel the wings in his throat an hour later when he wakes. The black birds have scattered and he stretches each leg before he stands. The rats are still boisterous, almost begging to be caught, but he lifts his head to sniff the wind. Pumpkin innards are delicious, but food out of the can is better. He turns his back on the rats and heads toward home.

His leash trails behind him as he retraces his steps, sniffing the urine he left on most signposts, revisiting his favorite trash cans and yards. Every house smells unique—this one like laundry, that one of wood smoke, another resplendent with spices and meat. One of his favorites sports a carpet of fragrant lavender that was swarmed by bees in the heat of the day, but which now is befouled by the stench of the ginger cat.

She crouches amidst the lavender, her yellow eyes gleaming at him in the dark. She doesn't budge when Toby steps toward her, not even when he growls. It's almost as if she doesn't fear him at all, which deepens his growl but also gives him pause. He freezes with one paw in the air, watching, waiting, until she bends unconcernedly to lick her fur.

He charges.

She is gone in an instant, down the street and around the corner, but it takes him only a few long strides to catch up and nip her tail. The taste of her makes him salivate; he barks victoriously until she rounds on him in a hiss. She turns from prey to predator in one quick motion, tail stiff, spine lined with razor-sharp fur, and he retreats in confusion.

"Bella!"

The man with the hose hobbles toward them, wielding a cane. Toby expects a welcome spray of water, so when the cane comes down hard on his back, he's more surprised than hurt.

"You get out of here!" the man yells, swinging the cane in the air in a wild game of fetch. Normally, Toby would leap at the chance to play, but the ginger cat is still hissing and beyond her Lola is in her nightgown, shuffling down the steps of her house.

Though the man with the cane calls her name, there is never any doubt that Toby will reach her first. He greets her on the sidewalk and noses her bony hand. She may smell like nothing, but he'll happily lick her anyway.

"Lola," she says, and taps his head.

She doesn't wear shoes, and she likes the mailbox as much as Toby does, running a finger along the red metal flag while Toby pees on the base. The man with the hose makes a racket coming after them, panting and smacking his cane against the ground, but Lola ignores him and turns her head up toward the stars. With all the street lights, there are never as many here as there are in the backyard, and maybe that's why she's crying. Maybe she can't see them, the same way he can't smell her. Maybe she wishes the man with the hose would leave her on the fence, where she wants to be.

By the time the man reaches them, Toby spots the ginger cat sitting smugly on the front porch. Toby lets out a deep grumble before the man jabs him in the chest with his cane.

"I said go! Leave us alone!"

The man takes Lola's arm, but it's a while before she'll even look at him. She drops a hand to Toby's neck and when she says, "Lola," he wags his tail. She squeezes his fur, then allows the man with the hose to lead her back into the house. It isn't until the door is closed that Toby feels the pain in his back and chest, but also realizes how close he is to home. A quick trot around the corner, then he's skidding onto Good Boy's front porch. The light is off, and when he scratches at the door, no one answers. He lays down on the mat, raising his head at every rustle.

The list of things he loves keeps getting longer:

Rats.

Pumpkin innards.

Lola.

Not only everything outside the front door, but everything within.

A welt rises where the man with the hose struck him and the porch mat is a far cry from Good Boy's bed. Tired and hungry, Toby has scratched the paint off a good portion of the door, but still Good Boy doesn't come. Two people argue in the house across the street; when he barks, the only answer is from a dog halfway down the block, then another farther than that.

He stays until he can't be alone any longer, then walks the three blocks to Sunshine's house. He finds the dog beneath the tree, whimpering as Toby approaches. The dog turns submissively onto his side to let Toby sniff two angry burn marks above his shoulder, along with the stench of the dark man's hands on his fur. Toby's hackles rise, but beneath the dog's foul scents, Sunshine is warm. Toby lies beside him and licks the dog's wounds.

Sunshine dozes as the moon rises and whines in his sleep. His dense, matted fur makes a comfortable pillow, but Toby doesn't close his eyes. He watches the occasional car pass and sniffs the air. He is aware of every movement, from the flutter of leaves to a mole descending back to safety to the dark man opening the door and stepping onto the porch.

Someone inside says, "You'll never do it," and the dark man, stinking of smoke and beer, sways and laughs. He walks inexpertly, hands out in front of him as if the world keeps rearranging itself, and Toby gets to his feet, his black coat blending into the shadows. He blinks at the flash of sharp metal in the dark man's fist, stiffens when the hard tip of the man's boot collides with Sunshine's ribs. The dog scrambles awake, yelping and choking himself on his rope in his panic to escape. The dark man wobbles, but the knife in his hand is steady. If he had the eyes of a dog, he'd have seen Toby stalking him long before he hears his growl.

The dark man freezes as Toby's lips curl. No matter how fast the dark man is, Toby is faster, and he never second-guesses what he knows. Some people smell of kindness and others of rot, and dogs have only seconds to tell the difference.

"Whoa," the dark man says, holding up his hands. "Jesus."

The dark man retreats a step and Toby crouches, ready to spring. Good Boy isn't there to tug him back or distract him with the desire to please. The dark man retreats a step, and Toby crouches lower, following. A trickle of sweat slides down the dark man's brow, Toby's legs tremble with the urge to spring. Sunshine's whimpers sound faraway, but the stench of terror is overwhelming. A vein pulses rapidly in the dark man's neck. Toby's gaze never leaves that target, even as two men emerge from the house.

"So?" the biggest one says, taking a long swig from a bottle. "You chicken out?"

The dark man points his knife at Toby and for a moment nothing happens. Then the man runs.

"Get in the house!" he yells.

Toby gives chase, but stops short of leaping and sinking his teeth into the man's neck. It's enough to watch him flee, pushing the other men through the door and slamming it behind them. Still, Toby throws himself against the door with a satisfying thud. He barks and scratches at the wood until the men stop shouting and slivers come off in his claws.

Then the world slowly returns. He shakes himself, front to back, while Sunshine lies down in the dirt. He steps off the porch to sniff fresher air and notices the scent of far-off rain and fallen leaves. Something musky walked through the yard earlier, probably a raccoon who beat him to all the good trash in the alley cans. And just beyond Sunshine's tree, he makes out the faint but distinctive aroma of bubblegum.

LOVE!

Nose to the ground, Toby tracks her—across the street, past the scarlet tree, up to the porch of the white house, then around the corner. She had been following him, but gave up in the alley, when she must have watched him rocket out of sight. Toby sniffs a weathered fence, and a dog on the other side greets him with a series of unimpressive woofs. Toby jams his nose under a broken slat and nips at a pair of black and white paws.

Then the paws retreat. A door slams and a boy says, "Hey Pearl, whatcha barking at?"

There is the swish of something flying through the air and the dog's clumsy gallop after it. Toby wags his tail and crams his nose beneath the fence to try to spy the game. He can't see anything but grass, but what he smells is heavenly—spun sugar, moldy tennis balls, and a rubber toy that squeaks when the dog bites into it. He hears the enviable sound of a dog being pet, along with her satisfied moans.

"That feel good, Pearl?"

Toby pulls his head out of the hole and leaps. On his first try, his head easily clears the top of the fence; the second time, he launches half his body into view. He glimpses the dog—black and white, insignificantly sized —and a boy, perhaps not even taller than he is. He jumps once more, but at the same time the gate latch clicks and the boy steps into the alley. He has dark hair and large, brown eyes, along with the kind of padding around the middle that makes a perfect pillow. The dog comes out after him, female and timid, with yellow goop at the corners of her eyes.

"Wow," the boy says. "You're big."

Toby turns from the fence and leaps on the boy, taking them both to the ground with a nice, cushy thud.

"Aaaaaaaa!" the boys says, wriggling and laughing as Toby licks his cheeks. "Aaaaaaaa! Aaaaaaaa!"

Aaaaaaaa tastes like he's been dipped in sugar. Toby gets lightheaded licking his arms; there is chocolate sauce behind his ear. Toby buries his nose in the boy's sweet neck, then nuzzles the fireplace of his belly, and instead of shoving him off, Aaaaaaaa throws his feet into the air in ecstasy. Once Toby gets his fill, he climbs off and displays his best skills, running down the alley, catapulting over trash cans, turning on a dime and charging back. Even for him, he reaches a speed that dazzles.

Aaaaaaaa applauds, so Toby does it again. Goopy Eyes barks at the dust storm he kicks up, while Aaaaaaaa raises a fist and yells, "Charge!" After a dozen laps, Toby performs a sliding stop and leans proudly against Aaaaaaaa, panting.

"Wow!" Aaaaaaaa says, giving him a sweet, sticky hand to lick. "We gotta go in now. You should come."

Yet another of Toby's favorite things is other people's backyards. He's broken through half a dozen gates to find fish ponds, fire pits, and once an entire table of meats and cheeses to devour before a group of women in funny hats ran him off. So when Aaaaaaaa opens the gate, Toby blasts past him and Goopy Eyes to find a magnificent yard of waist-high weeds inside. The ground is bedazzled with plastic army men, a half-chewed flip flop, and enough gopher holes to mine for days. He hears the rodents beneath him, unaware of his digging skills, and smells the smorgasbord of food the family had for dinner. He's certain this day can't get any better, until Aaaaaaaa puts a pudgy hand on his head and nudges him toward the house.

"You gotta be quiet, okay? If Mom finds you, we're dead."

5

No one does the dishes in Paradise.

Aaaaaaaa giggles as Toby licks his way across the unwashed dinner plates, gorging himself on half-eaten potatoes and gristly meats. There are buttery bread crusts and globs of creamy gravy, a mutilated masterpiece of graham cracker crumbs and fudgy goo. Aaaaaaaa drinks a glass of milk then holds out the cup to Toby, laughing as Toby slurps most of the contents onto the floor. Even the things Toby can't swallow taste delicious —bright curtains infused with years of perfume, a messy line-up of sweaty shoes, coffee cup rings, spilled wine across a tabletop.

Aaaaaaaa leads Toby and Goopy Eyes up the stairs and into a room that is as sweet-smelling and soft as he is. Toby leaps onto a sea of blankets and stuffed animals no one has ripped the stuffing from yet. He scoops up a fuzzy blue ferret and leaps onto the bed with it, digging out a spot in the tangled sheets where he can tear out the button eyes. Aaaaaaaa laughs and helps Goopy Eyes onto the bed beside him, while Toby thumps his tail against the wall. An answering thump comes from the other side.

"Shut the hell up, dirtbag!"

Aaaaaaaa grimaces as he lunges for Toby's swishing tail. "That's Chloe," he whispers. "She's a nightmare."

Toby easily evades Aaaaaaaa's grasp, smacking his tail even harder against the wall as he nudges the ferret into Aaaaaaaa's tiny hand. The boy isn't half as strong as LOVE or Good Boy, but he's quicker to take up a game of keep away. Aaaaaaaa grabs the ferret tightly, his round face turning pink as he tries desperately to hang on. Toby allows him a few futile yanks, then easily wrests the ferret from his hands and thrashes it in his teeth.

"Aaaaaaaa!" the boy says as Toby leaps victoriously from the bed to the closet door and back again. He perfected high-speed turns in his cell, but with an obstacle course of pillows and stuffed animals to navigate, playing the game here is so much better! He skirts a purple beanbag chair before twisting in mid-air, knocking over a lamp just as a teenaged girl throws open the door.

She is slender and hard-edged, with fur-like, spiky hair nearly as red as Good Boy's roses—the ones the man cordons off with chicken wire, which makes it hard, though not impossible, for Toby to dig them up. Her fingers sport black claws and when he leaps at her, she growls and slams a shoulder into his chest like the beefy, joyless bulldog who thinks he rules the dog park. He yelps as he falls backwards and hesitates before getting back up. Her scent confuses him—more human than canine, but not by much.

"Oh my God," she says, glaring at Toby, then turning her gaze to Aaaaaaaa. "You are so dead."

Aaaaaaaa grabs a blue blanket and tucks it beneath his chin. "Nah-ah," he replies.

Dog-Girl shows her teeth. "Mom will *murder* you."

She is dressed all in black from her lipstick to her shoes, which makes the green eyes she narrows at Toby almost as startling as her hair. She's like no other dog or girl he's seen before. When she grabs him by his harness, he considers challenging her, but quickly thinks better of it and lowers his head.

"Don't tell Mom," Aaaaaaaa says.

"She doesn't even like Pearl coming inside. You think she's gonna let you keep a monster like this?"

"He's not a monster!"

"He's somebody's pet, you moron. Have you even checked his tag to see who to call?"

Aaaaaaaa sits on the bed, quiet.

"Dumb ass," Dog-Girl says. She twists Toby's harness, which makes him flinch before one of her sharp fingernails scratches the itch that is always underneath. He turns slightly with a moan, to give her better access. He tries to chew up the harness every time Good Boy leaves for the day, but so far he's only managed to mangle the annoying, clanking tags.

As Dog-Girl looks at his handiwork, he tentatively licks her wrist. Her skin is as unusual as the rest of her—a mix of vinegar and musk, not altogether pleasant. But she keeps scratching him under the harness strap, so he doesn't pull away.

"The tags are all bitten up. I might be able to make out a license number, but I'm not hunting down the owner of some stupid stray."

Toby dares the slightest tail wag. There is dirt beneath her black fingernails, as if she's been digging up roses too.

"So you won't tell?" Aaaaaaaa asks.

"What's it worth to you?"

A tall, skinny boy passes down the hallway then doubles back, his lips moving but no sound emerging from his lips. His hair is the same vibrant shade as Dog-Girl's, but scrunched beneath enormous, black headphones. He glances at Toby, then lifts one of the headphones to let a deep, disembodied voice into the room.

"Yo," he says, "that's a dog."

Dog-Girl releases Toby's harness and sneers. "No shit, Sherlock."

"Yeah, *Sherlock*," Aaaaaaaa says.

Sherlock slips the headphones down around his neck, where the music continues to pulse: Dub du-dub du-dub du-dub. With a quick glance at Dog-Girl, Toby ambles forward, catching a whiff of ripe, unwashed armpits, another of his favorite things.

"Whoa, dog," Sherlock says as Toby sniffs his best parts, then throws his paws around the boy's shoulders to lick the speckles from his face.

"Bru, get off."

Sherlock pushes him to the ground, but Toby is tall enough to jam his nose right into Sherlock's magnificent armpit. The boy wears a long-sleeved shirt despite the warm night, the fabric under his arm sweat-stained and ripe. Sherlock twists away and climbs atop the desk chair.

"What the hell is his problem?" he asks.

Dog-Girl laughs as Toby circles the chair. "Maybe you're his type," she tells him.

"Yeah, Sherlock," Aaaaaaaa says. "His type."

Toby forgoes Sherlock's armpits once he gets a whiff of his feet. The boy doesn't wear socks and his toes are as spicy as black licorice.

" . . . Mom know he's here?" Sherlock is saying, balancing on one foot then the other, trying unsuccessfully to evade Toby's tongue.

"Oh yeah," Dog-Girl snaps. "Just like she knows about the goats we keep in the closet."

"Goats," Aaaaaaaa says and laughs.

Sherlock shoves Toby's nose away. "Gawd, would you stop?"

Dog-Girl steps into the hallway and cocks her head. "Did you hear that? She might be coming out of her drunken stupor."

Sherlock glares at her. "She's not drunk."

Dog-Girl waves a hand and returns to the room. "High on crack then. Whatever."

"She's sad," Sherlock says, his skinny arms dangling well past mid-thigh, like gangly tree limbs just asking to be torn free. "Give her a frickin' break." Toby mouths one of his bony wrists just as footsteps start up the stairs.

Toby smells the sudden tension; even Aaaaaaaa's sugary scent ferments. Suddenly Goopy Eyes, who's lain all but invisible in the folds of Aaaaaaaa's sheets, leaps toward the window and breaks the silence with a howl. Toby follows, barking because she barks, and because the sound of two dogs is always better than one. He scratches at the glass even before he sees the shadow sitting in the boughs of the scarlet tree.

"Shut up!" Dog-Girl shouts. "Oh my God, would you fucking shut up?"

Toby barely registers Dog-Girl's hands yanking at him. It's right there! Something darker than darkness, closer to the house than it was before.

He turns to fly down the stairs, but a wild-haired woman bars his way. She stands in the doorway, pink creases along one side of her face, staring at him as if he's the shadow in the scarlet tree, the thing that shouldn't be. He doesn't sense violence, but neither is she someone he'll lick without pause. She smells sweet and sour all at once, as if what's inside her has no correlation with what she pretends to be. When she steps into the room, everyone retreats.

She slowly scans Toby from top to bottom, as if he's monstrous-sized, a beast. Toby returns to Aaaaaaaa's side and presses himself against him.

"Take some time with your story," she says, "because I'm expecting it to be good."

Toby and Goopy Eyes sleep in the yard. Or, rather, Goopy Eyes barks at the shadow while Toby dozes, and while Goopy Eyes sleeps, Toby attempts to scale the fence. The shadow sits motionless just beyond it, in the lowest branch of the scarlet tree. It resembles a tall and broad-shouldered man, but its chest never rises or falls, nor does Toby smell anything other than the tree beneath it and the rank owl who nests above. It could be human, if humans were ever silent. Normally, they breathe and gurgle and gnash their teeth; even their dreams are full of sighs and swallows. On a quiet night, Toby can hear them sleeping through their walls.

Toby takes his turn barking, but the shadow is as impervious to noise as it is to wind and fatigue. Fifteen minutes later, Toby relents and sits quietly by the fence, keeping one eye on the shadow and the other on the house. Dog-Girl paces past an upstairs window; the wild-haired woman sits at the kitchen table with her head in her hands. The shadow swivels almost imperceptibly to watch them.

By daybreak, Toby is stiff and the shadow is fading—one of its wrists turns darker than the other, a knot in the scarlet tree becomes visible through its kneecap. When the sun clears the horizon, the shadow vanishes, and Toby finally succumbs to sleep. He dreams of wrestling with Good Boy and a litter of red-furred puppies, but wakes to something even better—Dog-Girl sitting beside him with a slice of cooked bacon in her hand. Toby eats the treat in three bites, then noses her fingers and pockets to find more.

"Don't be greedy," she says, pushing him away.

Giving up on the food, Toby trots around the yard, even more delighted with its contents in the early light of day. The Great Dane-sized weeds contain not only army men and gopher holes, but a rusting teeter-totter, sand buckets and broken frisbees, along with no less than a dozen tennis balls that have all lost their fuzz. He excavates a yellow plastic shovel that he easily snaps in two. The only part of the yard he doesn't care for is the tidy bed of flowers by the back door. With the shovel handle still in his mouth, he wanders over and takes a swipe at the dirt before Dog-Girl comes after him and yanks him by the harness.

"Stupid dog."

She tamps down the earth and inspects the flowers for damage, then heads toward the house. She doesn't stop Toby when he follows; she even lays a hand on his neck.

"Don't get too comfortable," she mutters. "This is the part when you die."

The wild-haired woman doles out food to everyone but herself. Toby eyeballs the plates of crisp bacon and gooey fried eggs, but can't make a move with Dog-Girl gripping his harness. This would aggravate him more if there weren't so many people around him. They talk one on top of the other like a pack of barking dogs.

"Mom, he's got a tag on so he's got to belong to somebody."

"Why can't we keep him, Mom?"

"Please, Mom? Please?"

"Mo-om!"

Mom pours herself coffee but doesn't drink. Extra bacon and eggs lay heaped on the stove, and Toby's tail wags as he ponders breaking free from Dog-Girl to snatch it. Mom attempts to twist her hair atop her head, but misses the long spirals by her ears. A few of her fingernails have splotches of pink; there are purple half-moons beneath her eyes. It's another perk of paradise, everyone wearing colors he can see.

"Absolutely not," Mom says. "One dog is more than enough." She takes a mound of dough out of the refrigerator and slaps it down on the counter.

"But Mom . . ." They all bark at once, which diverts Dog-Girl's attention long enough for Toby to break free. He snatches three slices of bacon and instantly swallows them whole, expecting Dog-Girl to smack him on the nose. Surprisingly, though, she doesn't touch him. She merely watches as he moves on to the eggs, one corner of her mouth turning up in a smirk.

Mom shakes her head and kneads the dough. Her fingers move mesmerizingly fast, rolling out dough, sliding one cookie sheet into the oven while taking another out, rinsing her hands and slicing vegetables which she throws into a pot. She smells of dough and bacon and beef and cream, and though she hasn't smiled at him yet, she makes Toby think of every treat he's ever eaten. He steps a little closer, just in case one of her delicacies slips to the floor.

Only Aaaaaaaa savors the morning meal, biting into a sticky bun coated with gooey white icing while Sherlocks puts on his headphones and Dog-Girl tosses her uneaten eggs into the trash. Mom glances at Toby but doesn't pet him, not even when he discovers a splatter of bacon grease on her pants and licks it clean.

" . . . I have to do," she says as she adds carrots to the pot. "If one of you would like to help out around here, this might be a different conversation."

Dog-Girl scoffs as she puts her plate in the dishwasher.

"Do you have something to say, Chloe?" Mom asks.

From the neck up, Dog-Girl is even paler today than she was yesterday, except for the black rings around her eyes. She slams the dishwasher door shut before Toby can lick the plates.

"Nope."

Mom sets down her knife and turns toward Dog-Girl. "Go ahead. I'm listening."

Aaaaaaaa manages to eat the sticky bun with one hand while pulling his blue blanket over his head with the other.

Dog-Girl rolls her eyes. "Yeah, right."

"Listen, young lady, I—"

"*I* do the dishes!" Dog-Girl shouts. "That includes your seven wine glasses every night."

The voice inside Sherlock's headphones gets louder. " . . . killin' my vibe . . .brought in alive . . ."

" . . . not going to dignify that statement," Mom says. "You know very well that the moment I come home from work I start cook—"

"No one's asking you to cook twenty meals a day!" Dog-Girl says. "You're the one making Jack fat."

"I'm not fat!" Aaaaaaaa replies, returning the last bite of sticky bun to his plate.

When Mom's hands tremble, she hides them behind her back where Toby can easily nibble her fingers. He's encouraged when she doesn't immediately shove him away.

"Anything else?" she asks.

Dog-Girl shrugs. "I'm not going to Stanford. It's a bunch of snobs there."

Everyone shouts at once then. Dog-Girl is the loudest, but Mom shows more flair, throwing her delicious fingers into the air. Sherlock yanks his headphone off his ears while Aaaaaaaa hurtles himself into his mother's arms, all of which creates the perfect opportunity for Toby to dig into the trash can and gobble up the remains of Dog-Girl's breakfast.

" . . . can't believe you . . . after everything . . . tutoring, the scholarship application I helped you w—"

"Right," Dog-Girl says. "Cuz it's about you."

"How can you even say that?"

When Mom's voice wobbles, Toby looks up from the trash. People say a lot of words when they're yelling, when all they really mean is *I don't like you anymore*. Aaaaaaaa pulls his blanket down over his eyes as Sherlock storms out the back door.

"Nothing's about me since your dad died," Mom says, swiping tears off her cheeks. "I'm just trying . . . never go out, never . . ."

Dog-Girl is unfazed, breathing as calmly as a pit bull who never loses a fight.

"Oh yeah, I forgot. You're the only one who lost Dad."

"Stop it," Aaaaaaaa says from beneath his blanket.

Dog-Girl shrugs. "I'll stop when she admits she's got a dozen bottles of vodka in her room."

When Dog-Girl turns her back, Mom slumps against the counter. From beneath his blanket, Aaaaaaaa is crying now too.

Mom puts her arm around Aaaaaaaa's shoulders. "It's okay," she says. "Everything's okay."

Dog-Girl snatches her backpack and stomps to the back door. It's only when she pauses that Toby's hackles rise. He moves cautiously to her side, and she puts a hand on his back while opening the door. They both know what's there, even if the others see nothing but sunlight and shadows. Dog-Girl lifts a hand and the shadow raises its own to meet hers. Toby throws back his head and howls.

The shadow vanishes instantly and Dog-Girl walks boldly through the place where it was. But there are goosebumps on her arms. Mom grabs Toby's harness and pulls him away from the door.

"What is wrong with this dog?" she asks.

To quiet him, they offer more bacon, which he eats distractedly while keeping his gaze on the open door. He resists all attempts to drag him outside until Goopy Eyes charges past, biting one end of a rubber snake. Toby watches her slide harmlessly across the patio, then he finally takes a few tentative steps outside.

The yard is free of shadows, but Toby still can't shake the growl in his throat. Mom walks Aaaaaaaa outside and locks the door behind her. "I'll call the shelter from work," she says. "The pound will be best . . ."

Aaaaaaaa ties his blanket to Toby's harness until it billows around him like a cape. Toby stumbles on the fabric, and by the time he chews himself free, Aaaaaaaa and Mom are gone. A car door slams; even the branches of the scarlet tree are deserted. Toby scouts gopher holes while Goopy Eyes sits by the fence and whines. There are at least a dozen rodent dens to excavate, but for the moment Toby decides he'd rather lie in the dirt beside Goopy Eyes, where he can rest his chin on the dog's warm leg.

There are better places, certainly—hundreds of them—but as always he'll pick the one with someone in it.

6

An hour's rest and Toby is ready to scout. First priority is excavating gopher holes, followed by locating and exhuming every last daffodil bulb in the flower bed by the house. As an unexpected bonus, the bulbs serve as the ceiling of a rabbit burrow, allowing him to get his jaws inches from a few furry necks before the terrified beasts bolt. The yard is a dog's dream of buried treasure—chicken wings, a decaying shoe sole, and a rusted spoon he'll chew for hours.

When the noon sun beats down, he flops onto his belly and paws lazily at a razor-straight line of ants. Twice, the doorbell rings and he and

Goopy Eyes go wild, but no one visits except for a magpie who screeches more nonsense than LOVE. Toby watches the back gate for signs of Dog-Girl or Aaaaaaaa, and sometimes even hopes a trick of the light will turn into a shadow. But it isn't until late afternoon that he leaps to his feet, head and ears forward, listening. Leaves crunch on the other side of the fence: An intruder!

It could be the tobacco-scented mailman or the woman who drives the big brown van he's jumped into twice! Goopy Eyes makes futile attempts to leap above the fence line, but Toby merely hoists his front paws onto the railing and peers over. Instantly, he thumps his tail madly.

LOVE! She stands a few feet to the right of him, one eye pressed to a hollowed out knot in the cedar planks. Her bubblegum scent makes the other side of the fence smell like heaven. When he whines a greeting, she turns sideways, not seeing him at once. Then finally she raises her gaze.

"Perro estúpido!" she says, her face breaking into a wide grin. "We'vebeenlookingeverywhereforyou!"

He dances on his hind legs as she maneuvers through bushes to reach him. "Mr. Thiery!" she yells. "Over here!"

She is too short to do more than raise a hand and tickle his chin with her fingers, but his dance quickens when he spots Good Boy running across the street. Good Boy! Where has he been? At the sight of him, Toby remembers everything he misses—the big, comfortable bed and his hedgehog and the bathroom game with Good Boy every morning and evening. His greeting is more like a cry as Good Boy fights the shrubbery to get to him.

"Toby," Good Boy says. He is tall enough to clear the fence and take Toby's face in his hands, brushing the caked dirt from his nose. "Do you know how worried I've been?"

"I can't believe he's right here," LOVE says. ". . . thought he'd be miles away by now."

Toby licks Good Boy's face, forgetting the rats and the dark man, even the banquet of food on Mom's counter. Good Boy tastes less like soap than ever before, and though Toby's back legs ache, he doesn't drop from the fence, not even when he hears the gate creak open and Aaaaaaaa come charging through. Nor when Sherlock, Mom and Dog-Girl follow, and Mom stops in her tracks to say, "Oh."

"Don't be startled," Good Boy says, scratching Toby's ears as he peers over the fence. "This is my . . . "

At Dog-Girl's shout, Toby senses the danger, but Good Boy is with him so he merely drops his tail. He rarely understands what he's done wrong, but he does know that the quicker the pain comes, the sooner he might be forgiven. He takes the blow to the side of his head and knows it's not as hard as it could be, but even so, everyone yells. Aaaaaaaa yanks Dog-Girl's arm, Mom comes running, and somehow Good Boy launches himself over the fence to stand beside him, which is well worth Dog-Girl grabbing him roughly by the ruff of the neck and baring her teeth.

"You. Stupid. Shit!" she screams. "Look what you've done!"

There's no fix for being hated. When Dog-Girl shoves him, Toby falls to the ground and exposes his belly, but even total submission isn't enough.

"What's wrong with you?"

"Stop it!"

"Let him go!"

He cowers when someone takes hold of his harness, but he quickly recognizes Good Boy's gentle fingers as Mom leads Dog-Girl away.

"Chloe, calm down," Mom says. "My God."

Dog-Girl glares at her, then presses her fists to her eyes. Hatred makes her smell far more human than canine.

"That was Dad's garden," she says.

Good Boy crouches beside him while LOVE cries on the other side of the fence.

"It doesn't matter," Mom says. "You don't hit—"

"He dug up the flowers I planted for him, Mom!" Dog-Girl shouts.

Good Boy's lips stretch into a thin, white line as he runs his hands over Toby's fur.

"Chloe," Mom says, quieter. "Please."

Dog-Girl drops her fists, revealing tear tracks that turn her white cheeks pink. Even at a distance, Toby trembles at the fury in her eyes.

"You're okay," Good Boy says. "Let's get up, boy."

He nudges Toby to his feet as Dog-Girl storms into the house. Mom raises a hand toward Good Boy, then lets it drop.

"I'm so sorry," she says. " . . . my daughter . . . planted for her father. He passed away last year."

Toby buries his nose in Good Boy's palm. Despite everything, the man has never smelled this delicious before, his sweat a pungent mixture of vinegar and salt. Good Boy swallows repeatedly, as if he's got mothballs in his throat.

" . . . very sorry," he says, his voice scratchy. " . . . my fault he got loose."

"Of course it isn't!" LOVE says from the other side of the fence.

Sherlock stands slightly apart, dressed for another season in jeans and a turtleneck sweater. He presses his headphones to his ears, as if he could block out the world and take the music inside him. But he looks up when LOVE finds something to stand on and hoists herself high enough to see over the fence.

"Finalmente!" she says, her curly hair studded with leaves.

"This is Sylvia," Good Boy says. "She walks Toby when . . . I'm Walter . . . down the street."

The sweat goes clear up Good Boy's arm, turning most tangy inside the arm of his shirt. Good Boy pushes him away, but Toby comes right back again, jamming his nose up as high as it will go.

"Alicia," Mom says. "This is Max and Jack. Sorry to say you've already met my daughter, Chloe."

Her gaze skips from garden to tree to Good Boy, which makes the man swallow again. Sherlock slides his headphones down around his neck, and Toby cocks his head at the deep, disembodied voice singing, "Yeah, wait. Yuh, wait."

" . . . going to take him to the shelter," Mom says. "I figured he was chipped?"

Sherlock takes a step, not noticing one of Toby's new holes. His ankle twists and he stumbles sideways, his knee slamming into the ground before he rights himself.

"Womp, womp," Aaaaaaaa says, and he and LOVE laugh. For the first time since everyone arrived, Toby wags his tail.

Sherlock's face reddens as he rushes into the house. Toby hears him pounding up the stairs, his music trailing behind him, "Yuh, ay ay."

"Anyway," Mom says, "I'm really glad you . . . not up to having two dogs."

She laughs, but there is no joy in it. Just like she cooked all that delicious food, but didn't eat a bite. She's here but not here, more solid than the shadow but not as interested in being alive.

"I'm up for it!" Aaaaaaaa says, wrapping his pudgy arms around Toby's neck. He squeals gleefully when Toby licks his face.

"Well," Good Boy says, picking up Toby's leash, which has been trailing after him ever since he ran off and is coated in burrs and gutter water and some fantastically fragrant green slime. "Thank you for taking Toby in. I'm sorry again about . . . Toby is . . . no idea what I was getting myself into."

It's the most words Toby has ever heard Good Boy speak, and every syllable turns the man's cheeks redder.

Toby finds his rusted spoon as Mom escorts him and Good Boy to the gate. Aaaaaaaa watches them go, stabbing a long stick into one of Toby's more extravagant excavation sites. It's an excellent stick, maybe even better than a spoon, and if Toby is quick, he's confident he can snatch it With a sudden pivot, he manages three steps back before Good Boy yanks hard on his harness.

"For crying out loud, Toby!" Good Boy shouts. "Haven't you had enough fun already?"

As Good Boy drags him to the gate, Mom laughs and brushes her fingers across Toby's fur.

"He's certainly a handful," she says, with a smile.

Good Boy opens the gate and shoves Toby through. "Worst dog I've ever had."

7

That night Good Boy opens not one, but two cans of food! And as if that isn't enough, he scrapes his leftovers into Toby's bowl—a delectable slop of beef stew and mashed potatoes. It is so delicious Toby has to lie down to eat. He licks the bowl clean half a dozen times before Good Boy walks to the bathroom.

Toby leaps to his feet and trots after him, delighted to be back in the tiny room where every move brushes him against Good Boy. His chew towel still hangs on the rod and tonight instead of glaring at the mirror, Good Boy drops to his knees. Toby wags his tail ferociously, knocking the soap dish off the counter as he licks first Good Boy's face, then his ears and neck. Good Boy raises his hands to ward him off, but there's no oomph in it. Toby even manages to knock him sideways and climb into his lap.

"Jesus," Good Boy says. "Stop."

Good Boy pushes Toby away, but a second later he draws him back. Toby wags his entire backside; he loves bathroom time and Good Boy's hugs and how everything in Good Boy's house is always the same. Good Boy buries his face in Toby's fur before slowly getting to his feet. Then he opens the cabinet, pours three pills out of a bottle, and swallows them without water.

"Shut up, Toby," he says.

Toby and Good Boy play everything from steal-the-shoe to tug-of-war, but Toby's favorite game by far is not bringing back the ball. Later that night, Toby snatches one of Good Boy's slow lobs out of the air and takes a victory lap around the backyard. It's a new ball, so after he dodges Good Boy's hand he lies in the cool grass to break it in. Good Boy puts his hands on his hips, but Toby merely rips out strips of yellow fuzz as the woman on the fence glows. She looks cool and distant, like she's taken the moon inside her, but when she smiles at Toby, he gets to his feet. With barely a stretch, he drops the ball into her shimmering lap, but she doesn't catch it. When it plinks off the edge of the fence, Toby wags his tail to retrieve it, then drops it into her lap again.

The woman on the fence hums, but not like most people. The sound is less a melody than the swooshing of wings. Her moonlit skin is as crinkled as old leaves, and there's a lifetime of scent ingrained in her gnarled fingers—sweat, blood, saltwater, polished wood and motor oil, Thanksgiving turkey and homemade birthday cakes, one man's shaving cream, potting soil and cat fur and tears—as if she's never washed away a single thing she's touched.

"Hello?" Good Boy says. "Are we playing or not?"

Toby inhales the bittersweet aroma of the woman's knuckle and Good Boy throws up his hands. There are scents Toby can't identify in the woman's wrist and elbows, a surprising coolness near her middle where most people are warm. Good Boy says something, but when Toby sniffs the woman's skirt, his nose scratches the fence post instead. The ruff on his neck rises, but the woman on the fence hums like mourning doves, and he joins her with a howl.

Good Boy tries to shush him, but it's the hard spray of water in his face that does the trick. Shock stuns him for a moment, then he drops to the ground to play. The man with the hose stands on a ladder in his yard, waving the hose wildly while Toby tries to catch the spray in his mouth. Every time the man yells the spray zigzags; on Toby's turn, he twists and leaps to bite the water from the air. Good Boy gets to his feet and comes running; the woman on the fence claps her hands and laughs.

Then it's done. The man with the hose grumbles, his hands trembling as he lowers the spray to a trickle. The woman on the fence reaches out to him, but he acts as if she's not even there.

"Mr. Pratt," Good Boy says, "what—"

The man with the hose points the nozzle at Toby, but disappointingly nothing comes out. "He woke my Phyllis! I shouldn't have to listen . . . barking day and night . . ." He flicks the hose with each word, but still nothing comes Toby's way but a few flecks of water.

"It was just a couple of barks," Good Boy says. "I wouldn't . . ."

"You've got no control over him," the man with the hose says. ". . . beast nearly killed my Bella yesterday! There's a law against dogs at large, you know."

The more he speaks, the more he trembles. He grips the top of the ladder for support, and the woman on the fence looks at him fondly.

"Toby got loose from his dog walker," Good Boy says. " . . . promise you . . ."

The man with the hose shakes his head. "You can't promise me anything. What if he comes after Phyllis?"

"Toby has never come after anyone," Good Boy replies. "He's exuberant for sure, and too big for his own good, but . . . "

" . . . animal that bites, chases or harasses a person must be put down within five days. That's straight from the city."

"Mr. Pratt, please."

The woman on the fence tries to stroke the old man's cheek, but she misses him by inches as he climbs down from his perch. Toby can no longer see him behind the fence, and the glow around the woman on the fence is fading too.

"If that dog comes near us again," the man grumbles from his yard, "I'm calling the pound."

The next time LOVE arrives, she holds a shiny, industrial-strength leash.

"See this?" she says, twining the leash around her forearm before latching it to Toby's harness. "Justtrytogetawayfrommenowmister!"

Once outside, Toby confirms that no one has stolen his half-buried bone beneath the bougainvillea before lunging excitedly at a woman in a bright blue jogging suit, who squeals and runs away before he even has the chance to lick her.

"Settle down, monster," LOVE says.

Toby wags his tail and drags LOVE down the street. He identifies the scents of four women, seven men, and five dogs who marked the nearby lamppost, including the horrible golden Lab and another in heat. Toby lifts a leg to reclaim his territory before turning the corner and heading toward the ginger cat's house. The feline is nowhere to be found, but Lola is inside, sitting blank-faced by the window. Her gray hair is unkempt, her skin no longer lit up by moonlight. Toby drops his tail, but LOVE urges him onward.

"Don't let that man see you," she says. "You're public enemy number one."

They continue down the road, following a slow-moving truck to the end of the block, where three men unload rolls of green grass onto the curb by Aaaaaaaa's house. Goopy Eyes barks from behind the fence, but when Toby heads in that direction, LOVE tugs him back.

"Not again, buddy," she says, leading him instead up the path toward the dark man's house.

Sunshine is down to six inches of freedom—barely enough to growl when Toby trots up and nips his tail. It's a mediocre game at best, but Toby still bobs and weaves, slapping a paw over Sunshine's shoulder and snatching the dog's well-chewed stick. He expects at least a retaliatory bark, but Sunshine merely sinks to the ground and whimpers. Which is when Toby smells fire and the dark man steps onto the porch.

Toby's fur bristles, but LOVE's senses are dull. She tosses her curly hair and takes a step toward the house.

"Toby loves to visit your dog," she says.

The dark man shrugs. "Take them both. Do me a favor."

LOVE's laugh is louder than usual, but the dark man doesn't smile. "I can barely handle him," LOVE says. "The other day he . . . looking for hours . . . We got—"

The dark man steps off the porch while she's still talking and walks past her without a glance. But he keeps his distance from Toby, who curls back his lips and snarls.

"Toby!" LOVE says, snapping his leash. "Stop being a jerk!"

LOVE tries to follow the dark man to his truck, but Toby won't budge. Just because he runs toward most everything doesn't mean he's blind to the few things he ought to avoid.

"Come on!" LOVE says, futilely yanking Toby's leash. The dark man lights a cigarette and opens the door to his truck. LOVE glares at Toby, then calls out, "Um, what's your name?"

The dark man exhales a white cloud of smoke and flicks ashes onto the hood of his truck. "Colby," he says.

"I'm Sylvia. It'snicetomeetyouofficially."

The dark man stares. "Look," he says finally, "if you're gonna come around, you need to ditch the dog."

LOVE glances at Toby. "I've got to walk him. It's my . . . maybe later?"

"Forget it," the dark man says, and climbs into his truck.

As he guns the engine, LOVE rolls up and back on the balls of her feet. For a moment, Toby thinks she might run, but as the truck pulls away she sighs and goes still. Sunshine doesn't stop trembling even after the truck turns the corner. It takes two treats from LOVE's pocket to begin to calm him, even though Toby never shook at all and he only got one! LOVE pets them both while the workmen across the street roll wheelbarrows of sod into Goopy Eyes's backyard, the shadow overseeing the work from the tree above.

LOVE stays unusually silent, except for the occasional sniffle that makes Toby lean into her until she stumbles and laughs. As her arms come around him, he noses around in her pocket for his share of the biscuits.

"Monster," she says with a smile.

On the dying woman's front porch, Toby and LOVE play a five minute game of tug-of-war, which of course Toby wins. He will not go inside, not with the stench of death permeating everything, not to mention the strong stink of cat. LOVE throws her arms in the air and walks inside without him, while he scans the building until he glimpses a pair of silver eyes watching him from the roof. Normally, he'd leap after anything feline, but the air feels heavy, like a wet blanket draped over house and yard. He hasn't heard a single bird since they arrived; there is only the sound of the woman dying inside—her labored breathing, the rattle of her lungs.

Toby steps off the porch and pads to the backyard with its one spindly tree. He scratches at the earth and, even in the hard-packed soil, quickly excavates a foot-deep hole. He doesn't stop when it begins to rain, or even when he hears LOVE crying. The deeper he digs, the more luscious the soil, until it is cool as ice on his paws and squirming with worms.

When the hole is deep enough for an animal to die in, he sits beside the grave and howls. The rain is unpleasant, but the dying isn't done. It bleeds from the house and spooks the worms underground; the cat sits vigil on the corner of the roof like a silver gargoyle. LOVE comes out to tell him to hush, but rushes back inside when the dying woman calls her. When LOVE opens the door once more, she is cradling the old woman in her arms.

Toby howls once more then goes silent. The dying woman is child-sized now, wrapped in a musty, brown blanket that he doesn't want to sniff further. Her patchy gray hair pokes out of a woolen cap and her eyes are milky; she looks past Toby as if something far more interesting is standing right behind him.

"Es esto mejor, mamá?" LOVE asks.

The woman's foggy eyes gleam. "Sí."

LOVE sits on the porch step, the woman tucked against her chest like a newborn. There is no sound but the dying woman's rasping and the plinking of rain on the earth. Toby doesn't like the smell of the blanket, but he pads across the soggy yard and wedges his face between the two women just the same. LOVE pushes away his muddy snout, but the old woman can't escape so easily. The fetid blanket falls away and, beneath it, the dying woman smells like the earth he just dug up, moldering into something rich. Toby licks her from cheek to cheek.

"Puaj," the dying woman whispers. "El monstruo."

She closes her eyes and the cat springs from the roof, marching so boldly onto the stoop that Toby steps away. The cat watches Toby steadily, then lies down at LOVE's feet as if Toby is no more menacing than a flea. A small tuft of fur rises on Toby's back, but somehow the growl never comes. Instead, the rain fills his hole with water, the woman's chest rises and falls and doesn't rise again. LOVE weeps as the first robin returns to her perch on the lonely tree.

More birds come. A second robin, then a pair of iridescent grackles who scatter when the rain turns to hail. The barrage is so loud that the cat blinks and LOVE raises her face long enough for Toby to lick her too. He doesn't mind the saltiness of her tears, because beneath that he still tastes bubblegum and soda pop and everything else he adores. LOVE puts a hand on his neck and draws him closer.

"Good boy, Toby," she says. Good Boy!

8

Good Boy sleeps Toby's way now—in fits and starts throughout the night, then dozing at mid-day and after dinner. Toby prefers napping when the sun shines through the window, but if Good Boy wants to close the blinds, that'll work too. A quick game in the bathroom, followed by a few laps around the backyard, then Good Boy barely grunts when Toby jumps into bed beside him. Tonight, he doesn't even wake when the doorbell rings.

Toby leaps from the bed, barking well before he reaches the living room window where he spies Mom standing on the porch. She balances a round, chocolate-frosted cake in the crook of one arm while ringing the doorbell with the other. Not only a visitor, but a visitor with dessert! Toby races back to Good Boy's bedroom, ignoring the no-jump zone to leap onto the man's chest. Good Boy comes alive with a grunt of pain and bloodshot eyes that open less than halfway.

"Ugh," he grunts, while Toby sprints back to the front door. When Mom stops ringing the doorbell, Toby flings himself at the living room window, scraping his nails down the glass. Mom glances at him nervously before stepping off the porch.

" . . . s'kay," Good Boy says, stumbling into the living room, one hand clenched on the edge of the couch, the other in a fist over his eye. "Coming." He fell asleep wearing his work clothes, which still had a tissue in the pocket that Toby ripped to shreds.

Yet another of Toby's favorite games begins the moment Good Boy cracks open the door. The man contorts his body to form a blockade while Toby dances, trying to find a way past. One of Toby's most cherished victories came via a bold leap over Good Boy's hip to land on the man who delivers his dog food, but today he drops to his belly and torpedos beneath Good Boy's outstretched leg.

"Look out!" Good Boy shouts.

Mom turns just before Toby reaches her and, with surprising quickness, hoists the cake above her head. With half a leap, Toby could easily reach it, but he's satisfied with simply jumping on her chest. She's been cooking more than cake—her collar smells of barbecue, two flecks of dried gravy garnish her chin. She doesn't dance with him the way LOVE does, but when he licks her, she tastes like the best meals he's ever had in Good Boy's kitchen, which the man usually brings home in a bag.

"I'm so sorry," Good Boy says, yanking Toby down.

"It's okay," Mom says, lowering the cake. "It's nice to get a greeting like that once in a while."

Toby goes in for another lick, but Good Boy tugs him back. "Stop it!" Good Boy says. "For God's sake."

"Really, it's all right," Mom replies. " . . . for you. My backyard . . . how to thank you. You didn't have to do that."

Good Boy relaxes his grip on the harness just enough for Toby to press his backside into Mom's legs.

"Well . . . after what Toby did to . . ."

"I just couldn't believe it," Mom says. "The garden and the lawn When I came home . . . sent a whole crew!"

"They work for me . . . I didn't mean to overstep."

Mom balances the cake in one hand and squeezes Good Boy's arm with the other. "It was incredibly generous."

Good Boy stiffens suddenly and Mom drops her hand. Toby feels the heat of her through her clothes and wags his tail.

"Well," she says, holding out the cake while Toby licks the lotion off her ankles. "It's red velvet with chocolate frosting. I wasn't sure . . ."

Toby freezes at the sound of rustling in the bushes. He raises a paw but neither Mom nor Good Boy notice the speckled head and black eyes of the nighthawk. Good Boy accepts the cake, talking right over the bird's nervous chirps.

"This looks amazing," he says. "You didn't have to . . . hoping Chloe liked the new flowers."

"She did," Mom says. "She didn't even mind that they weren't black."

When they laugh, the nighthawk takes flight. Toby leaps for it, his shoulder grazing the cake in Good Boy's hands before the man yanks him back once again. Good Boy sets the cake on the porch bench—minus the portion that Toby licks from his fur.

"Well, I'd better—"

"W-would you like to come in?" Good Boy asks.

"Oh," Mom replies, "I should probably get home to the kids."

Good Boy steps back abruptly, pulling Toby with him. "Of course Thank you so much for the cake."

As Good Boy gathers up the smashed cake, Mom lifts a hand toward him then lets it fall. The nighthawk circles overhead, squawking about its freedom while Toby allows himself to be led inside. Good Boy pauses in the entry, closing his eyes while Toby wags his tail. Between Mom and the bird and a mouthful of cake, the evening has been outstanding! To top it off, Good Boy heads down the hall to the bathroom for the second time in one night.

Toby snaps up his hedgehog and trots after him. Instead of standing by the mirror, Good Boy sits on the rim of the bathtub—the perfect height for Toby to jam the hedgehog into his lap. Good Boy holds the toy listlessly while Toby rips at the stitching, his tail swatting the bottle of pills from the counter. Good Boy lurches as the pills scatter, dropping to his knees so Toby can easily lick his ears.

"Toby, stop!" Good Boy yells, grabbing pills from behind the toilet while Toby nuzzles his neck. Good Boy picks the last pill out of a lint-filled corner and swallows it without taking a drink. There is still cake and they haven't even gone for their nighttime walk yet! Every time Toby thinks life can't get any better, it does.

Seconds after Good Boy's car exits the driveway every morning, Toby hears LOVE's key in the lock. These days they only take short walks around the block, but now that LOVE stays with him all day, Toby tolerates the lack of exercise. And she lets him lie beside her on the couch! While she naps, he sniffs her face and hair, trying to locate all the scents that have gone missing. The bubblegum aroma was the first to go, followed by grass and soda pop and disinfectant, and now there's nothing left but clove cigarettes. She stays all day and speaks little nonsense. Sometimes she wakes up crying and hugs him until he squirms.

LOVE likes opening closets and cupboards to examine their contents. She's especially fond of a half-filled book of photographs Good Boy keeps in a bedside drawer and his many bottles of pills. She prefers the food in the back of the pantry, and after she eats something she rearranges soups and cereal boxes until the shelves look fuller than before. She doesn't like to soil Good Boy's trash bins, preferring to toss her empty containers into the neighbors' bins in the alley. Afterwards, she sits against the fence in the backyard for hours, lighting cigarette after cigarette and blowing smoke at the moonlit woman who lounges above her and doesn't seem to mind.

Today, LOVE doesn't say a word as he rips branches from Good Boy's wisteria and chews them down to pulp. The woman on the fence ignores the constant smoke in her eyes, humming softly and reaching down to stroke LOVE's curly hair. LOVE never acknowledges the old woman's presence, but as afternoon turns to evening she sighs and closes her eyes. She doesn't move again until Good Boy pulls up in the driveway, then she and Toby race for the entry. Toby wins by a mile, but LOVE still smiles for the first time all day.

"Had a great, long walk with Toby," she says. "Be back again tomorrow!"

After she leaves, Toby jumps right up onto the couch.

"No!" Good Boy yells. "Off."

Toby lays his chin on the arm rest. Words mean more on some days than others, and luckily today Good Boy shows no sign of backing them up. The man shakes his head and walks into the kitchen while Toby dozes; an hour later, Toby wakes to darkness and an odd breeze in the house. He climbs off the couch and stretches, following Good Boy's trail to the bathroom (he missed the game!) and on to the open back door. The man's scent leads to the grass and no farther, perhaps because the woman on the fence no longer hums. She merely sits on the fence, glowing more like stars than the moon now, still brilliant but distant and cool. When a pair of bats flitter overhead, she raises her arms as if all she wants in this world is to follow them into the sky.

Back inside, Toby trots down the hall to the bedroom, where he finds Good Boy asleep in the big bed. Toby climbs up next to him, circling the blankets until he finds the perfect hollow to curl up along the man's warm flank. Good Boy doesn't grumble or push him away, not even when Toby licks a cheek before closing his eyes. Toby sleeps in short spurts when Good Boy's chest rises and falls slowly, then wakes when the man's breathing goes still then stutters back.

In the morning, when the alarm sounds, Good Boy does not get up. The phone on the nightstand lights up, chirping and vibrating incessantly as Toby nudges Good Boy's chin with his nose, but the man won't budge. Nor does he wake at the sound of LOVE's key in the lock, or her voice calling out from the other room.

"Mr. Thiery?" she says. "Toby?"

Instead of going to greet her, Toby lies down flat and rests his chin on Good Boy's chest. A few moments later, LOVE walks into the bedroom, where the phone still chimes and Toby doesn't lift his head. "Mr. Thiery? Walter?"

She approaches the bed slowly, then her voice grows shrill. She shakes Good Boy by the shoulders and presses her ear to his chest. Toby watches her without moving as she turns off the alarm and runs to the bathroom, returning with Good Boy's pills and her phone to her ear. Her words spill out in a torrent, and Toby doesn't bother to make them out. She paces while he tries to slow his breathing to match Good Boy's. Every few seconds, he feels like he's underwater. Even the sound of a siren nearing the house hardly registers. Then strange voices call out and two men in matching blue clothes rush into the room.

When Toby growls, they stop and hold up their hands. LOVE hurries to Toby's side and wraps her arms around him. The moment she attempts to slide him from the bed, he shows his teeth.

"Perro loco," she says, crying as she lays her body on top of his. He squirms to get free as the men who smell even soapier than Good Boy squirt something pungent up Good Boy's nose. One of them puts a mask over Good Boy's mouth and nose and LOVE cries harder.

"Come on, man," the man says. "Time to wake up."

Toby wriggles out from beneath LOVE's body and, with a snarl, flushes the men back to the door. He positions himself between them and Good Boy, teeth bared. Everything in the room smells wrong, either sterilized or foul.

The men dare a step forward, but before Toby can challenge them, Good Boy opens his eyes. Toby barks joyfully as Good Boy looks around the room in panic.

"You're okay," one of the men says. He glances at Toby, then takes another step forward and turns over Good Boy's wrist, placing his fingers atop the blue veins. "It's the Narcan we used to wake you up."

"You're all right, Mr. Thiery, ohmyGod!" LOVE exclaims.

Toby thumps his tail and licks Good Boy's face until he dislodges the mask.

LOVE yanks Toby away again as the men replace Good Boy's mask and ease him onto a gurney. By the time Toby emerges victorious from the tussle, the men have wheeled Good Boy out of the room and closed the door. Toby scratches at the wood, while LOVE merely stands there, talking to the men through the wall. When she finally opens the door, Toby barrels into the living room to find it empty. His mouth is so dry it feels as if his tongue is made of sand. LOVE collapses on the floor beside him. He waits for nonsense, but she has nothing to say.

Hours later, LOVE tries to coax him onto the couch beside her, but Toby sleeps by the front door. In the morning, she brings him a plate of scrambled eggs that turn his stomach.

"Come on, Toby," she says.

Every time a car door slams he looks out the window, but Good Boy doesn't return.

It's one thing to stay alive and quite another to put effort into living. Toby remembers his first days in his cell—how his body soldiered on even when his heart wasn't in it. Some mornings he'd lie listlessly on the concrete floor and not even bark when a collie walked past. Once, he went four days without a bite of kibble and never felt a moment's hunger. In fact, the less he ate, the more alluring his dreams—whole nights when he could run as far as he wanted and still come home to people who didn't leave.

So when Good Boy does not come home, Toby survives. He stops eating and drinking and sits by the window, watching the people on his street who survive too. The teenager who ogles warm houses, but sleeps in a battered Mustang. The middle-aged woman who drives round and round the block, as if there's nowhere she really wants to be. The couple who walk the street together every evening but never speak. Even LOVE, who forgets to go home, and who has stopped eating too.

LOVE lets Toby into the yard twice a day, but rarely throws the ball. She's content to sit on the patio while he tries to tunnel beneath the fence, unearthing rootballs and a concrete footer and making the old woman above him sway. The woman on the fence's lifetime of scents have shrunk to three—grassy fields, lemonade, and baby oil, as if she's been running around like a child again, going back in time. She alone seems to savor the crisp fall days, still stretching her arms toward the sky. The man with the hose swipes a broom across her lap to clear the debris, and she laughs when crimson leaves swirl around her. She never eats or drinks either, but in her case this only makes her more radiant, as if she's feeding off something even Toby can't see.

When LOVE leads him back inside, Toby resumes his position by the window while LOVE lies on the couch. She stopped turning on the television days ago. She is amazingly adept at sleep.

She is snoring when her phone rings, but unlike Good Boy, she comes fully awake with a start. While she speaks, Toby rests his chin on the windowsill, though there is no one to watch. He hears a car in the distance, but it never comes closer. Even the golden Lab has been absent lately, not even bothering to soil the yard.

Then suddenly LOVE bolts from the room and returns quickly with a bucket and mop. The moment Toby smells the scent of soap, he turns away from the window. For the first time in days, he feels a stab of hunger as he trots across the wet floor.

"TobyohmyGodwouldyoustop!" she says.

Every push of the mop makes the house smell more familiar. Toby follows LOVE's dance through the kitchen and hallway, stamping his paws with the lemony scent. By the time they reach the bathroom, his stomach is rumbling. He laps up the toilet water until LOVE pushes him aside and uses a bristly brush to clean the bowl. He licks her neck happily as she squeals and scrubs the bathtub. In all the commotion, neither of them hears the front door open or the footsteps in the hallway until Good Boy is right there.

Life comes roaring back with a surge of hunger and a whooshing in Toby's ears. He flings himself upwards and sideways, colliding with Good Boy's chest. But the man is ready, with both feet braced against the doorway and his arms opened wide.

"I'm happy to see you too, boy," Good Boy says, getting a hand beneath Toby's squirming hind legs and holding him tight.

Toby makes sure he licks everything, from eyebrows to chin whiskers to the briny spot behind the ears. LOVE stands beside the bathtub with a dripping sponge in her hand. She and Good Boy both glance at the medicine cabinet, then Good Boy untangles Toby's paws and lowers him to the floor. Toby circles him until he finds the angle that will give him the most contact, fur to skin, leg to leg.

"I could have come to get you," LOVE says.

Good Boy shakes his head. "You've done enough. I want to apologize . . . to find me that way . . ."

"It's okay," LOVE tells him. "I'm just glad you're all right."

Good Boy glances at his reflection in the mirror. "Nothing about this is okay."

Toby thumps his tail against the vanity. He could run for miles, but instead he wriggles between Good Boy's legs.

"Mr Thiery—"

"Walt," Good Boy says, stumbling sideways as Toby plows through him. "Please, at this point, you really need to call me Walt."

There is little room in the bathroom to maneuver, which means that, no matter which way Toby turns, he touches both Good Boy and LOVE at the same time! He worms his way back through Good Boy's legs as the man shuffles into the hallway, LOVE following close enough behind that Toby's tail swishes her knees. Good Boy picks up Toby's hedgehog and says, "You want this? You want it?" Then suddenly all the pressure on Toby's chest eases. He lunges for the toy and shakes it in his teeth until the last of the stuffing bursts free. Good Boy grabs one end and drags Toby into the living room, where the man sinks into the sofa where LOVE has been sleeping for days. LOVE glances at the dozen cigarette stubs crushed into a mug on the coffee table, then perches on the arm of the chair.

"Sylvia," Good Boy says, "I really am so sorry."

"No, Mr. Thi—"

Good Boy raises his hand. "Please, I need you to know. I never meant . . . horrified that you had to . . . Can you ever forgive me?"

With three quick tugs, Toby yanks the hedgehog from Good Boy's grip, then immediately tosses it back in the man's lap. Tail wagging, he retreats a few steps, trying to anticipate where the toy will fly. But instead of throwing it, Good Boy twists the hedgehog's limp torso in half and holds it tight.

"There's nothing to forgive," LOVE says.

Good Boy's shoulders slump. He drops the hedgehog at his feet, which is hardly worth Toby's effort to snatch it. Still, he plops himself down on the floor to chew his prize while Good Boy takes money from his wallet.

" . . . for spending so much time with him," he says. "Your mother must be missing you."

"Mr. Thiery—"

"Walt."

"Walt," LOVE says. "You don't have to pay me. My mom . . . My mom died."

It's the sudden quiet that makes Toby raise his head. LOVE stares at her hands while Good Boy doesn't know what to do with his—reaching toward her one moment, then clenching his fists the next.

"Oh, Sylvia," the man says. "I had no idea. When?"

"A couple weeks ago."

"My God, I'm so sorry. I wish I'd . . ." Good Boy runs his fingers through his hair and stares at Toby, who finally rips the second ear off his hedgehog and thumps his tail. "What must you think of me? You've been going through all this while I can't even manage . . ."

LOVE sniffles. "You have pain too. It's not a competition."

Looking more decided now, Good Boy leans forward and takes LOVE's hands between his own.

"I am truly sorry," he says.

"It's okay. She's been sick a long time."

"It was just you and your mom, wasn't it? Where will you—"

"My uncle took me in," LOVE says quickly, pulling her hands away. Toby licks her ankle when he feels the sudden heat of her. "Areyougonnabeokay? Like, with the pills?"

Good Boy stands and walks to the window. "I don't think I know what okay is . . . lost my wife seven years ago. Afterwards I just couldn't face . . . no excuse."

"Mr. Th—Walt, that's terrible."

"It was a long time ago," Good Boy says without turning around. "Then I hurt my back . . . the pills made me numb, inside and out . . . such a relief, I can't even tell you."

Toby leaves the remains of his hedgehog to join Good Boy at the window. At last there is some activity! A squirrel scrambling up the oak tree and a deliveryman bringing pizza to the teenager in his car.

"How will you stop yourself?" LOVE asks.

Good Boy turns around. "I don't know."

A pair of robins rustle through the bougainvillea and Toby hoists himself onto the windowsill for a closer look.

"Toby, down!" Good Boy says. He swats at Toby's chest, which isn't nearly enough to knock him back or stop him from scratching at the glass and flushing the birds. Satisfied that he's secured the yard, Toby trots back to LOVE and presses himself against her knees.

"Well," Good Boy says.

"He's just used to me. He's been moping the whole time you've been gone."

Toby moans as she scratches the itch in his ear, while Good Boy glances at the crushed cigarettes.

"I shouldn't have smoked in the house," LOVE says, pulling away from Toby to pick up the ashtray and take it to the kitchen trash can.

"It's okay," Good Boy calls after her. "There are worse vices."

By the time LOVE returns, Good Boy is pacing. Toby follows him from window to sofa and back again, cutting him off at the turns.

"Toby, move!" Good Boy says. LOVE is oddly silent, which makes Good Boy talk more and more. ". . . obviously need to work on some things . . . the hospital social worker . . . never thought I'd need . . . take some time off . . . rest and therapy . . . maybe more time with Toby is the key."

He laughs hoarsely as LOVE gathers her things—phone and keys, clothes thrown over the back of the wing chair, shoes kicked to each corner of the room. She stuffs everything in a backpack, then heads to the door.

"So glad you have your uncle," Good Boy continues. "I'm sure he . . . Toby, stay."

Toby already has one paw out the door LOVE opens before Good Boy grabs him by the tail. LOVE blinks a few times before crouching down and kissing Toby's nose. When she steps onto the porch, Toby tries to follow, but Good Boy blocks him with an arm across his chest.

"I really can't thank you enough," the man says as Toby squirms.

LOVE smiles but walks strangely, with her arms folded across her stomach and a shudder every few steps. When Toby doesn't want to go somewhere, he widens his stance and plants himself low to the ground, but LOVE gets into her car and drives away. Good Boy waits until the car turns the corner, then tries, unsuccessfully, to coerce Toby back into the house. What Toby wants is to race that car until he catches LOVE; he wants to run so fast around the ones he loves that no one can ever leave.

But he also wants Good Boy to stop crying, so he licks the fresh tears from the man's cheeks. Good Boy clings to him, and Toby doesn't budge even though the stench of disinfectant is stronger than ever.

"That's my good boy," Good Boy says.

9

Bird!

On their twelfth walk in three days, thirteenth if you count the time Toby shot past the deliveryman and dove into the neighbor's swimming pool before Good Boy even left the porch, the robin stands mere feet away on the neighbor's lawn. Toby holds his breath and raises his right paw while the bird pecks unconcernedly at her worm. Then he charges, getting a brief taste of tail feathers before the robin takes flight.

"No!" Good Boy barks.

Good Boy yells more than he used to, but he usually holds Toby afterwards so there's no need to pay him any mind. In fact, the man's punishments have become so inconsistent that Toby tries his luck leaping on every stranger he meets. And while he can't squeeze into the tiny second bathroom Good Boy now frequents, the man makes it up to him by walking him multiple times a day. In the morning, Good Boy laces his sneakers and the two of them sprint. They race again at mid-day and, after Good Boy vomits up his dinner, they jog around the patio. Late at night, after Good Boy soaks the bedsheets in sweat, he paces the hallway while Toby nips at his heels.

After the robin disappears, Good Boy steps into the street to retch while Toby sniffs a sewer drain. When Good Boy sprints again, Toby gallops ecstatically beside him, nose twitching at a series of weedy lots teeming with gnats. Every time Good Boy stops to hunch over, Toby sneaks in a mouthful of grass. On the way home, they pass Sunshine, who thumps his thick tail before getting gingerly to his feet. But Good Boy ignores the big dog, keeping Toby on a short leash and crossing the street toward Aaaaaaaa's. As the evening shadows lengthen, one of them separates itself from the trunk of the scarlet tree.

The shadow is less corporeal than it was, with hair like black smoke and one leg so faint, lawn moths fly right through it. The shadow glides toward them and Good Boy hesitates, running a hand over the goose bumps on his arm. Shadow and man are roughly the same height and build, but when Good Boy steps forward, the shadow retreats. It watches them steadily as Good Boy pulls Toby toward the door, then fades into twilight. First it's there, then it's gone, and when Toby sniffs the air he smells only

Mom's cooking and the last vestiges of the morning rain. Good Boy wipes his palms on his pants, then raises a hand to knock.

A moment later, the door opens and Toby leaps onto Mom's chest. Her shirt smells like sausages and he manages to lick her wine-stained lips before Good Boy pulls him off.

"Toby, down!" he says. "I'm so sorry."

Mom glances at her fuzzy slippers, then kicks them off her feet for Toby to fetch. He instantly lunges for them, but Good Boy curses and yanks him back. Behind Mom, Dog-Girl freezes halfway down the stairs, dwarfed beneath a man-sized shirt with a black fist on the front. Her hair has been shaved so short, Toby can make out the freckles on her scalp.

"I know it's late," Good Boy says, wrangling him until Toby can do little more than lick Mom's toes. "I just . . . jogging this way . . . client cancelled on an order of sod . . . plenty to do your front yard too."

Mom moves her feet out of reach and tucks a curl behind her ear. "Oh, I couldn't possibly . . ."

"Jobs are scarce this time of year. You'd be doing me a favor . . ."

Dog-Girl leans forward slightly, the way the more aggressive dogs do when they see Toby's size. Toby steps between her and Good Boy, extending his neck to show his full height.

"I feel like we'd be taking advantage of you," Mom says. "You've already gone well beyond . . . This is too much."

Good Boy steps off the porch abruptly, dragging Toby with him while Dog-Girl smirks. "Of course," he says. "I totally understand. Have a good evening."

He and Toby are halfway to the sidewalk before Mom hurries after them "Walt," she says, "wait."

Across the street, Sunshine begins barking. Toby's nostrils flare at the scent of clove cigarettes and he turns in time to see LOVE disappearing inside the dark man's house. LOVE! He vaults toward her only to be unceremoniously tugged back.

"Toby, stay!"

Music erupts from the dark man's house and Toby strains against his leash. "For God's sake, dog," Good Boy says, grabbing Toby by the harness. "What's wrong with you?"

The music is shrill and hurts his ears; Sunshine barks even louder.

"Anyway," Mom says. "I didn't mean . . . I'm just not used to someone doing these things for me."

"I understand," Good Boy tells her. "It was just a thought. No pressure."

"Are you like the nicest person in the world?" Mom asks.

Good Boy laughs and shakes his head. "I very much doubt it."

"Well, you look that way to me." Mom glances at the scarlet tree, but there is no sign of the shadow now. "I'm not . . . since my husband . . ." She takes a deep breath. "Would you like to come inside? I've got wine."

She smiles, but Good Boy doesn't see it as Sunshine's barks turn to miserable howls. "That poor dog . . ."

When Dog-Girl comes charging out of the house, the fur on Toby's neck stands on end. But she storms past as if she can't see or smell them.

"Shut up, you stupid mutt!"

"Leave him alone," Mom says. "He's just barking."

"He's insane. I'm going—"

"I think that's Sylvia's car," Good Boy interrupts.

They all turn to look at the brown car parked in the driveway across the street.

"Your dog walker?" Mom asks.

"Of course it's hers," Dog-Girl snorts. "She's there all the time. Just ask Max."

Mom straightens. "I don't see what Max has to do with it," she says. "And anyway, it's none of our business."

Dog-Girl scoffs. "Tell that to Romeo."

"That's ridiculous," Mom says. "Max barely knows her."

"Just the way he likes it," Dog-Girl replies. "So she won't find out what a loser he is."

"Chloe . . ."

Their voices grow louder as Sunshine's howls turn hoarse. The dog's water bowl is overturned, and even from across the street, Toby can smell fresh blood beneath his collar. The dark man's house isn't lit up like all the others, but the thumping beat rattles the windows.

" . . . can't interfere!" Mom yells.

"Maybe *you* can't," Dog-Girl barks. Then she bolts across the street like a runaway dog, and Toby wags his tail.

"Chloe!"

This time, Good Boy doesn't hold him back when Toby leads the charge. Good Boy and Mom follow him across the street, reaching Dog-Girl just as she unties Sunshine's rope from the tree. When the dog doesn't budge, Dog-Girl knees him in the ribs.

"It's called freedom, stupid," she says. "Go!"

Sunshine cowers for just a moment, then suddenly he turns and runs. His rope trails after him as he plows over one of the dark man's lawn chairs and barrels down the street. Toby barks and springs after him, his harness cutting into his shoulder blades as Good Boy struggles to contain him.

"Whoa!" Good Boy shouts. "Toby!"

Sunshine disappears around the corner just as the dark man flings open his front door. His unbuttoned jeans rest precariously on his hips; he glances at the empty tree before turning to Dog-Girl, who smiles wickedly.

Toby stops lunging and stiffens, ears forward, but the dark man merely shrugs and disappears back inside the house.

"That guy's such a creep," Dog-Girl says.

"Maybe," Mom replied, "but that was his—"

"So you think it's okay to chain up a dog like that?" Dog-Girl asks.

Mom looks at Sunshine's overturned water bowl. "Of course not, but you can't just take matters into your own hands."

"Yes you can, Mom," Dog-Girl says adamantly. "You have to."

Dog-Girl stomps back across the street. Toby strains to hear Sunshine galloping in the distance, but the stench of blood and fear is fading fast.

"Got any kids, Walter?" Mom asks. "They're delightful."

"I was never that lucky," Good Boy says quietly. He hunches forward and Mom touches his hand.

"Are you all right?"

"Fine," Good Boy says. "Just getting over a little bug."

She doesn't let go of him right away, so she doesn't notice Sherlock creeping across their lawn until he reaches the shadows of the scarlet tree. The boy isn't looking at them either; his gaze never leaves the door of the dark man's house.

Good Boy hardly breathes. The hand Mom isn't holding reaches for Toby's neck and clutches him tight. Mom finally releases him and steps back with a nervous laugh.

"Well, I'd better check if Chloe set our dog free too."

She is halfway to the house when Good Boy finally takes a deep breath. "I'd really love to do that lawn!" he calls out.

When Mom turns around, her smile transforms her face. Even Sherlock seems startled, wrenching his gaze from the dark man's house to stare at his mother.

"If I agree," Mom says, "you have to come to dinner."

Good Boy's fingers on Toby's fur burn. "It's a deal."

For more than two weeks, Good Boy never leaves him, so when the man puts on his work boots and steps out the front door, Toby waits. He cocks his head, anticipating the sound of returning footsteps, and when they fail to come, he scratches at the door. By the time he hears the car pulling out of the drive, he's overturned a wing chair and peed on the rug. Last night Good Boy's nightmares still woke them, but instead of pacing, the man fell right back to sleep. Now Toby is the one who paces, following Good Boy's old route from kitchen to bedroom to den. He breaks into the pantry, but everything except impenetrable canned goods has been moved to the top shelf. Even lying on the couch fails to soothe him, so he jumps onto Good Boy's bed and chews the sheets.

He's reduced a pillowcase to tatters by the time a key turns in the lock. He freezes with a strip of flannel in his mouth, but it's LOVE who comes into the bedroom and opens her arms. Toby leaps from the bed, throwing his paws over her shoulders, and she holds him just as fiercely.

"Come here, you slippery fish," she says.

LOVE doesn't yell about the sheets or the urine, and after she puts on his harness, she lets him lead her wherever he wants. They zigzag along the best-smelling alleys and sidewalks until they reach the dog park, where

LOVE unclips his leash. Toby wastes no time leaping into the murky pond, then bowling over every dog half his size. LOVE waits patiently for him beneath a tree, not talking to the young mothers the way she usually does, smoking her clove cigarettes. When Toby finally trots to her side, she gets to her feet slowly. Then she takes him to the house where Sunshine used to live.

The dark man leans against his porch railing, dressed like any other man in jeans and a leather jacket but reeking of something wild. Across the street, Goopy Eyes whines on the porch while Sherlock ties his shoes. Music bleeds from the boy's headphones; he moves his lips silently until he spots the dark man lighting a cigarette.

Smoke obscures the dark man's face for a moment, but not enough to stifle Toby's growls. He once barked all night after a pair of coyotes invaded the yard, so when LOVE puts a hand on his head to shush him, he ignores her and howls instead. Goopy Eyes joins him, and while LOVE and Sherlock yell at them to stop, the dark man moves silently toward them and tosses his lit cigarette at Toby's chest. Toby barely notices the burn, but LOVE cries out and brushes his singed fur.

"What are you—"

"I hate that dog," the dark man says, matching Toby's snarl with one of his own before walking to his truck.

LOVE crushes the cigarette beneath her shoe while the dark man drives away. Goopy Eyes goes quiet, but Toby barks until the stink of exhaust fumes fades and Sherlock and the dog cross the street. The rest of the world returns slowly—Goopy Eyes sniffing his burnt fur, LOVE breathing shakily, the man in Sherlock's headphones telling them to "hol' up hol' up."

Sherlock silences his headphones and rolls up and back on the balls of his feet. He sneaks quick peeks at LOVE's face, as if the sight of her burns his eyes.

"Sylvia," he says, his voice breaking as if he's never said a word so loudly before. He is almost as tall as Good Boy, but half the weight, like a tree that hasn't gotten any sunlight.

LOVE's eyes are watery, but she doesn't cry. "He's not as bad as he seems," she says.

Sherlock stares at the dark man's house. "Why do you keep . . ."

LOVE waves an arm. " . . . nowhere else. This *is* home now."

They're silent for so long that Sherlock fidgets with his headphones. A few notes spill out, then a woman croons, "Yeah care for me, care for me," before Sherlocks shuts off the music again.

"You could stay with us," he says breathlessly, as if the words take all the wind from his lungs.

"Right. Your mom would . . . homeless Latina sleeping on her sofa."

LOVE laughs harshly and leads Toby away from the house. Toby glances back to see Sherlock watching them while Goopy Eyes licks the brown grass. They turn the corner and make it all the way to Good Boy's porch before LOVE's tears finally fall. She kneels on the concrete beside Toby, holding him so tightly he can barely lick the cocoa butter from her knees. When they head inside to the sofa, she invites Toby onto her lap.

It's a few perfect minutes while she sniffles and pets him, then she stills herself and takes out her phone. When the dark man's voice enters the room, Toby leaps off the couch, but there is no scent of fire. He would bark, but LOVE is crying again.

"All I'm asking . . . " she says, reaching for Toby and bending forward until she rests her cheek atop his head. " . . . please don't make . . . okay, if that's what you want."

Toby presses himself against LOVE until the dark man goes silent, and even then he doesn't leave. It's been years since he's had to survive in the wild, but he still knows when the situation isn't safe. One thing, at least, was easier when no one loved him: When he attacked the enemy, there was no one to tell him to stop.

10

The shadow on Aaaaaaaa's front porch is little more than a mirage now—a shimmer of a once strong man who winks out the moment Toby gets close. Toby sniffs the air, but deciphers nothing but the scent of new sod, along with a whiff of decay. His ruff doesn't even stand on end; when Mom opens the door smelling of pot roast, his tail wags right through the place where the shadow's knees ought to be.

"Come in!" she says. "I still can't thank you enough for this." She waves her hand at the newly green front yard, which Toby has already discovered is much harder to dig, and the mirage caresses her shoulder. Toby noses her skirt, then her bare knees and feet, but her toenails smell awful, like gasoline.

"You really want Toby in your house?" Good Boy asks.

Mom swats at her shoulder as if a fly has landed there. "Let's live on the edge," she says.

The moment Good Boy unclips Toby's leash, he charges into the family room and knocks Aaaaaaaa to the floor. The boy laughs when Toby pins his blue cape to the ground and licks the crusted sugar from his lips.

"Toby!" Good Boy says, but by then Toby has bounded onto the sofa, unseating Goopy Eyes before knocking Sherlock's headphones off his ears. A man chants, "Na Na Na Na Na" as Toby traverses Sherlock's bony lap. The boy never laughs the way Aaaaaaaa does, but he doesn't push him away either as he glances at the door.

"She's not coming, loser," Dog-Girl says.

"Na Na Na Na Na." Glaring at Dog-Girl, Sherlock shimmies out from under Toby's legs and heads toward the stairs. Dog-Girl snickers as she leans against the wall, once again draped in black from head to toe. There used to be only two kinds of people in the world—those Toby jumped on and the few, like the dark man, who he watched. But now there is Dog-Girl, who should not be approached. She crosses her arms and looks right past him, as if he's as insignificant to her as the weakest dog at the park.

"Whatever you're cooking smells delicious," Good Boy says.

"Oh, it's just pot roast," Mom tells him, walking into the kitchen. "Would you like some wine?"

She is already pouring two glasses when Good Boy says, "Actually, could I get a glass of water?"

Dog-Girl smirks. "More for you, Mom."

Mom's cheeks redden as Toby climbs cautiously off the couch. He keeps his head low as he crosses the room. He can feel Dog-Girl watching him, but he can't stop himself from lying at her feet. She is barefoot, a tattoo of a bleeding rose gracing her ankle, the bottom of her feet covered in dirt. She has the scent of a dog who won't sleep anywhere but outside. When she doesn't shove him away, he flicks his tail.

Mom walks back from the kitchen with a glass of wine and another of water and talks even more than LOVE. Dog-Girl sniggers as she runs a foot down Toby's back; he can't imagine a more perfect evening until Aaaaaaaa runs toward him holding a rubber hot dog over his head. Toby doesn't even have to stretch his neck to snatch it, or run very fast to keep the prize. Goopy Eyes slides across the hardwood floor trying to catch him, then knocks over a coat rack making a sudden turn. Mom and Good Boy both yell, but by then Toby and Goopy Eyes have found the stairs. The door to Aaaaaaaa's room is closed, but the next one flies open when Toby slams his body into it, revealing a thin, messy bed and gargantuan speakers.

"Hey!" Sherlock says, flinging himself from the bed as Toby and Goopy Eyes charge inside.

Toby immediately drops the toy. The scent of blood is fresh—a few specks smeared on the twisted bed sheets, a thin line oozing from the wound on Sherlock's arm. The boy's shirt is off, making it easy for Toby to lick the cut before Sherlock grabs him by the harness.

"Knock it off!"

"Max?" Mom calls from the stairway. Her footsteps approach as Sherlock kicks the door closed. For once, his headphones are silent. Toby can hear the beating of his heart.

"Are the dogs in there with you?" Mom asks.

"Yeah," he says. "They're fine."

The doorknob turns. "I can just come get—"

Sherlock releases Toby to slam his back against the door. "I said they're fine!" he yells. "I'm getting dressed, all right? Jesus."

The knob twists back abruptly as Toby licks the tally of pink and white scars. They go from wrist to elbow like a prisoner's tick marks, one for every day he's survived. Sherlock snatches a white hoodie from the bed.

On the other side of the door, Mom sighs. "Dinner's in five minutes," she says.

Sherlocks puts on the hoodie, yanking the sleeves down to his wrists, then turns the music on loud. He grabs the bloodied razor blade from the floor, turning away from Toby like a dog standing guard over a bone.

A deep-voiced man asks, "Who talkin' now? Who gon' stop me now?" as Sherlock drops to the edge of the bed. Goopy Eyes whines while Toby works his nose up under Sherlock's sleeve and runs a tongue across the battered skin. There's a dog at the park like that, covered in pink welts, whole chunks of fur missing. Even Toby doesn't go near him. But Sherlock's wounds are surrounded by freckles and wiry red hairs, and the longer Toby licks him, the less the boy shakes.

"Max!" Mom shouts from downstairs. "Dinner!"

Sherlock opens a drawer in the bedside table and drops the blade inside. Aaaaaaaa may be sweet and Dog-Girl the leader, but Sherlock is the one who sings.

"Who gon' stop me now?"

Goopy Eyes and Toby nab the most lucrative dinner locations—Goopy Eyes beneath the long table and Toby at Aaaaaaaa's feet. Goopy Eyes snags the most crumbs, but Toby scores the food Aaaaaaaa spits into his napkin— potatoes and carrots in a delectable gravy and half-chewed chunks of fatty beef.

Mom does most of the talking, and when there's a moment's silence, she laughs. Her hands never stop moving—passing out food, refilling glasses with water and her goblet with wine, running her fingers through her hair. Good Boy makes the occasional comment, to which Mom laughs even more, but Dog-Girl, Sherlock, and Aaaaaaaa say nothing. Sherlock spins his food around his plate; Dog Girl smirks and eats nothing but bread.

"... only thing was the call center," Mom is saying. "... a degree in marketing meant nothing ... housewife for 16 years."

"It couldn't have been easy for you," Good Boy tells her.

"Overwhelming," Mom replies. "A million things I never thought of ... couldn't take it all in ... not sick a day in his life until ... wouldn't believe the bills ... funeral arrangements, life insurance ... you want to die too but you can't."

It's when she goes quiet that Toby lifts his head. Then she gulps her wine and laughs oddly, like there's something stuck in her throat.

"Listen to me!" she says, waving her hand. "Tell me about you."

"Not much to tell," Good Boy says. "I've got my business. Lawn care, some commercial hardscapes. . . mostly mow and blow."

"You make things beautiful for people."

Good Boy smiles while Aaaaaaaa's napkin reveals a chunk of buttered bread. "You've made a beautiful home for your family."

"Oh, right. You saw the yard before you got here."

"That's just grass. The house, your amazing cooking . . ."

94

Mom shakes her head, and a strand of dark, wavy hair comes loose. "I cook when I'm stressed . . . make up new recipes . . . and I don't mind eating!" She laughs again and pats her stomach. "My divorced friends all got skinny . . . dress like teenagers . . . not sure why I can't . . . at least the callers can't see—"

"Mom, stop," Dog-Girl says, and Mom's smile fades. "You're not in eighth grade."

Mom studies the table, then gets to her feet. "Excuse me," she says and heads into the kitchen.

Sherlock shoves his plate away. "Why you always hatin' on her?"

Dog-Girl glares at him. "She's embarrassing herself. And so are you, white boy."

Toby knows, the moment their gazes lock, that Sherlock will be the first to look away.

"Whatever," the boy says and shoves back his chair. As he stomps from the room, Aaaaaaaa forgets to refill the napkin. Toby moves on to Good Boy's hand, but the man pushes him away.

"So your wife's dead," Dog-Girl says.

Good Boy flinches. "Yes."

Dog-Girl leans back in her chair. "My dad had metastatic colon cancer. Stage four when they found . . . your wife die of cancer?"

Good Boy blinks more than normal. "A car accident. Seven years . . . drunk driver."

Dog-Girl doesn't answer, but Toby still hears something in her throat, a cross between a whimper and a sigh, a sound maybe even she doesn't know she's making. She stabs her fork into a piece of meat on her plate then just leaves it there, and Toby flicks his tail. The amount of food she doesn't eat would keep him satisfied for days.

"It took my dad ten months to die," she says at last. "The chemo . . . looked like a freak by—"

"Don't," Aaaaaaaa says. For once, there is no smile on his face.

Dog-Girl waves him off and glowers at Good Boy. "People told us we were lucky . . . time to say goodbye. You think that's luck?"

Though he'd like to snatch Dog-Girl's food, Toby stays where he is, licking the hand that Good Boy clenches on his lap.

"No. I'm sorry about your dad."

"Mmm-hmm," Dog-Girl says. "And yet here you are. Hitting on my mom."

"That's not—"

Mom returns with a two-layered chocolate cake, and Toby immediately abandons Good Boy's hand to trot to her side. Whatever she did in the other room made her smell better; there's a fruity red stain on the front of her blouse and powdered sugar on her skirt.

"Who wants cake?" she asks. "I've got coffee going too."

No one says anything for a moment, then Aaaaaaaa hands Mom his plate. "The slice with the most frosting."

Dog-Girl scoffs. "You're going to be obese."

"Am not!"

"A seven hundred pound troll."

Aaaaaaaa sinks lower in his chair.

"Stop trying to scare your brother," Mom says. She hands Aaaaaaaa a thick slice, then looks at Sherlock's empty chair.

"Where's Max?"

Dog-Girl shrugs. "Probably French kissing his pillow."

Mom sits down tiredly in her chair. "Chloe Noel, would you please stop?"

Dog-Girl stares at her. "Stop what? Stating facts?"

"Stop trying to ruin our dinner."

Good Boy had been staring at the floor, but now he looks up. "That would be impossible," he says, and Mom smiles.

"Oh yeah?" Dog-Girl's eyes narrow as she looks at Good Boy. "Let me try harder. My dad put in that grass you ripped out. . . still sleeps in his clothes . . . this was his favorite meal."

Dog-Girl's language isn't exactly barking, but everyone still leans away.

"Oh my God, Chloe, please," Mom says, her voice cracking.

Dog-Girl braces her hands on the table and leans forward. "His name was Mike. In case you even care."

"That's enough, Chloe," Mom says. "Go to your room."

Dog-Girl stands so abruptly, she kicks over her chair. Mom blinks back tears as Dog-Girl stomps across the room and starts up the stairs, then turns and slams out the front door. Goopy Eyes quivers under the table, but Toby moves from Good Boy to Mom and lays his chin in her lap.

"Oh," she says, resting a hand on his head.

Good Boy talks gently, but Toby doesn't listen to the words. Mom barely moves her fingers, yet she knows exactly where to scratch. With her other hand, she pets Goopy Eyes until the dog's trembling subsides, then reaches across the table to smooth out Aaaaaaaa's cape.

"Go out and play, honey," she says. "Everything is fine."

Goopy Eyes follows Aaaaaaaa out the back door, but Toby stays inside until Mom's fingers go still. Good Boy lays his hand over hers, squeezing her fingers and not scratching Toby at all. Toby shakes them both free, then heads for the backyard, where the shadow curls up on a branch like a dying leaf and, in an upstairs window, Dog-Girl strikes the same pose. The new grass is a little spongy, but not enough to slow Toby down. In seconds, he laps Goopy Eyes and blasts through Aaaaaaaa's cape.

Aaaaaaaa laughs and yells, "Toro!" as Toby spins and charges back again. Considering everything, it is another perfect day.

The sun hasn't yet risen when a knock at the door jolts Toby awake. Barking wildly, he leaps from Good Boy's bed to the hallway and immediately howls with outrage. Somehow the stink of the ginger cat has infiltrated the house. Sliding across the hardwood floor, he presses his nose to the crack beneath the front door. She is right on the porch, contaminating everything! He can hardly breathe with the stench of her and races back to the bedroom for Good Boy. The man is still groggy, pulling on his robe. Toby runs circles around him, barking more warnings.

"Toby, quiet!" Good Boy shouts.

Toby barks even louder as he races Good Boy back to their prey. The moment the door opens, Toby lunges, but this time Good Boy anticipates the move and knocks him backwards with a shove of his shoulder. Disoriented, it takes Toby a minute to get back on his feet and make another fruitless leap. By then, Good Boy has blocked off all but a sliver of the doorway, though which Toby can make out the pinched face of the man with the hose and the foul-smelling ginger cat in his arms, hissing.

"Mr. Pratt," Good Boy says, "it's five in the morning. Everything all right?"

"Of course everything is not all right!"

The man with the hose clings to the squirming cat with one hand and jabs his cane in Toby's direction with the other. It's an exceptional stick, with the kind of dense wood that can be chewed for hours, but Toby can't bark and snatch it at the same time. The old man holds out the cat, who yowls wildly. Toby lunges once more, managing to wriggle his head past Good Boy's roadblock. The rest of him squirms in frustration as the ginger cat claws her way up the old man's wool coat.

"She's all bloody!" the man with the hose cries, wrestling the cat as she crawls across his shoulder.

Good Boy makes a sudden turn and shoves Toby backwards. "Enough!" he yells, ducking out the door and slamming it shut before Toby can dart through. Toby scratches at the wood, then runs to the window. Good Boy left it open just enough for Toby to ram his nose at the screen and knock it loose.

"Mr. Pratt," Good Boy says, "I can assure you it wasn't . . . always on leash."

" . . . no other dog would . . . "

The ginger cat leaps from the man's arms to the porch railing, then in one bound disappears over the gate to the backyard. Toby races in that direction, charging down the hallway toward the bedroom where he spies the cat through the window, scuttling up the wall and onto the lap of the woman on the fence. The beast curls up contentedly as if Toby is miles away instead of standing on his hind legs a mere twenty feet from her, barking madly to sound the alarm.

"Toby, knock it off!" Good Boy shouts from the other room.

Outside, the ginger cat purrs as the woman on the fence lifts her face toward the rising sun. Toby barks until the room grows brighter and the odor in the air begins to change. First, the scent of cat and soap is replaced by fresh cut wood and roses. Then suddenly the promise of rain and wet earth oozes out of the carpet, making the room smell more like outside than in. He follows the trail of scents around the room, getting a whiff of pine near the bedside table, rotting maple leaves hidden in the folds of the sheets. When he finally hoists his paws onto the windowsill, he sniffs the brine of the sea.

Outside, the woman on the fence glows so brightly now that, for a moment, he has to look away. When he turns back the light has dimmed and the fence is empty, except for the cat. Even the smell of rain is fading as the ginger cat paces atop the fence, her tail cleaning house, swishing away leaves and debris. Then she vanishes too, slinking down the other side of the fence.

Toby drops from the window and scoops up his hedgehog, carting it back to the living room, where Good Boy has cracked open the door.

" . . . won't tolerate it any more," the man with the hose is saying. " . . . with Phyllis . . . hospice . . . know what that's like?"

"Mr. Pratt—"

" . . . terrorize people . . . call animal control and have him euthanized. . . my word on that."

As the old man steps off the porch, the first rays of the sun fall on him too. But instead of looking up, he jams his cane into the earth and steps into the shadows grumbling, as if the last thing he wants is to start another day.

11

Toby still jumps on LOVE when she arrives every morning, but once she brings the leash, he hides.   Under the table is good, but in closets and beneath Good Boy's bed are better.

"It's called a walk, you dummy," she says whenever he refuses to budge.

They've stopped going to the dog park.   He hasn't run for days. Every morning is a repeat of the day before—after LOVE arrives, they walk the same two blocks, barely lingering over the familiar scents. Toby has tried bolting and tugging and lying down defiantly on the golden Lab's lawn, but there is no defense against the sausage-flavored biscuits that LOVE uses to bribe him. In the end, he will follow her anywhere, even if it's always to Sunshine's tree, where she ties him up.

Today, she lures him out of the broom closet with bacon strips. He drops his tail when she snaps on his leash.

"Come on," she says. "Don't look at me like that."

Once they're outside, he tries to head toward the dog park, but as always LOVE pulls him the other way. She hardly gives him time to sniff the ivy where the golden Lab peed or bark at a passing car before they end up back at the dark man's house.

He presses his face between her legs as she ties him to the tree.

"You're fine," she says. "I'll get you some water."

While she turns on the hose, he circles the tree looking for escape routes, which only tangles the leash and drives his harness painfully into his shoulder.

"OhmyGodToby," LOVE says, setting down his water bowl and pushing him in the other direction until his leash is slack. Then she touches his head briefly before walking into the house. Across the street the scarlet tree is empty; not even Goopy Eyes scratches at her fence. Toby lies down in the hollow Sunshine dug and drops his head on his paws. When he dozes, he dreams of slow-moving rats and ropes he can snap with his teeth.

He comes awake to a wiry brown tail whiplashing his face and Sunshine's dirt-caked nose in his groin. Toby leaps to his feet as Sunshine runs circles around him, the scent of fear that used to cling to the dog washed away by river water and sap. Sunshine nips his ear and Toby gets a whiff of pine forests and decaying fish, along with the worms Sunshine ate for breakfast.   His brown paws are studded with brambles, which don't seem to bother him in the least.

They dodge and weave, Toby coming up short against his leash while Sunshine's old rope trails behind him, black now, chewed and frayed. Sunshine drinks all the water, but he never turns his back to the house. He wrestles Toby until he hears the dark man's voice, then he bolts across the street, sprinting into the alley beyond Goopy Eyes's new lawn.

There is no sign of LOVE as the dark man emerges from the house. His boots have a metal toe that could kick a dog to death, but Toby still leans forward and growls.   The dark man narrows his eyes and lights a cigarette, as if he's never backed down either, no matter what it may have cost.   There's a collie at the dog park who's the same, attacking dogs twice his size as if he knows the first strike is the only one he'll get.   Toby stiffens his tail, waiting, but the dark man merely shakes his head and steps off the porch, keeping clear of the tree as he walks to his truck and drives away.

Toby watches the road until he's sure the dark man is gone, then he returns his gaze to the porch.   He pants as the sun grows hotter, ignoring the rustling of leaves and a school bus rumbling to a stop, even Aaaaaaaa running up the path to his house and calling out "Mom!" before he's even inside.   He listens only for the sound of LOVE's voice, even a whisper.   The muscles in his legs tremble with the strain of waiting for her to come.

An hour later, when she still hasn't emerged, his black fur is so hot not even horseflies dare to land on him.   He sniffs his dry water bowl, then tries to cool himself by rolling in the dirt.   Across the street, a car with duct-taped windows pulls to the curb and Dog-Girl and Sherlock get out. Sherlock glances Toby's way before disappearing into his backyard while Dog-Girl leans down to talk to the driver, a girl with an elaborate skull tattoo on a bare circle of scalp.   The music pulsing from the car is so jarring and loud, it shakes all that's left of the shadow from the tree.

As the car pulls away, the shadow flickers like a dying candle, like something even dogs aren't sure they see. It has no hand to move; it's Dog-Girl who reaches out then drops her arm quickly, as if she's been caught in a moment of weakness. When she turns and sees Toby, she glances once more at the scarlet tree, then crosses the street.

When she unties him from the tree, Toby adds her to the things he loves and licks her salty wrists. She grunts and shoves him away, but not before she grabs his leash and tugs him across the street. They head into her backyard, where Sherlock sits with his eyes closed, head bobbing. Dog-Girl slaps off his headphones and tosses the leash in his lap.

"Tell your girlfriend she sucks," she says.

After Toby licks the scars on his arms, Sherlock pulls on a musty brown sweater and leads Toby to the front yard. The boy sits on the grass, the man in his headphones chanting, "Oh, oh, oh, I does it, yeah," while Toby snaps at the white moths that hover above the lawn like stars.

When LOVE finally emerges from the house across the street Sherlock stays silent and rips clumps of grass from the ground. LOVE grimaces as she steps off the porch, then stares at the empty tree where she left Toby.

"Shit," she says.

Toby likes the song in Sherlock's headphones. There's a smile in the man's voice and a rhythm that makes his tail swish. Across the street, LOVE walks around the tree trunk as if Toby is pug-sized and could be hiding under a root. "Toby!" she shouts.

Toby takes a step toward her, but Sherlock puts a hand on his head. "I might," the voice in Sherlock's headphones says.

"Tobyyyyyyyy!"

Toby's name echoes down the street, maybe all the way to the ginger cat's yard. LOVE doesn't spot them in the darkness until she takes a few steps into the road.

"OhmygodToby," she says, holding her side as she runs toward them. She hugs Toby briefly before turning to Sherlock. "Why didn't you say something?"

She reaches for the leash, but when Sherlock doesn't return it to her, Toby sits by his side. It's one thing to love LOVE, but quite another to trust her. Not with the stink of the dark man still on her. Not when people, unlike dogs, fall out of love all the time.

Sherlock pulls his headphones down to his neck. "You keep tying him up to that tree," he says.

"Are you stalking me?"

She leans on her left leg as if her right one won't hold her, and Toby's nose twitches. She still sports a riot of scents, but now they're unpleasant—a mixture of sweat and beer and the blood seeping through her shirt.

Sherlock gets to his feet. "He hurt you," he says quietly.

LOVE puts a hand on her hip and glares at him. "So?"

A frog croaks from somewhere in the grass, or maybe from beneath the car in the driveway. They're never where Toby thinks they are. By the time he cocks his head, the sound comes from behind him.

Sherlock shakes his head and holds out his headphones to LOVE. "Don't bother," she says. "We don't have the same taste in music." Sherlock smiles with one side of his mouth. "Nah, but this is dope." He puts the headphones on LOVE's ears and mouths the words. *Fear. Lie. Never never never.* LOVE closes her eyes. *Worry. Bury. Never never.*

Love may be untrustworthy, but it also makes dogs and humans brave. When LOVE cries, Sherlock holds her and Toby wriggles into the warm spot between their legs. It takes a while, but eventually Sherlock squeezes her tight enough to push the bubblegum scent out through her pores. Toby wags his tail as the voice in Sherlock's headphones sounds like a heartbeat.

Give up. You can't. Never.

12

That night, Toby dreams he's a hundred feet tall and able to pluck hawks right out of the sky. The air is thin but intensely fragrant, as if every lover's bouquet and exhalation rises into the clouds and never dies. The woman on the fence soars beside him, riding the thermals while the ginger cat hisses from the yard below. Toby swipes at the cat with a massive paw and loses his balance, slicing clouds in half as he falls. When he finally opens his eyes, he's lying diagonally in Good Boy's bed, claiming all the pillows. The stink of the ginger cat fades as the aroma of coffee wafts in from the kitchen.

He stretches until he's as long as he can make himself, paws extending a good six inches over the corners of the bed. Good Boy left a slipper on the floor for him to chew, but as he climbs off the bed he hears clanking in the bathroom. The game is back on! He rushes into the tiny room, his tail sideswiping the line of plastic pill bottles Good Boy has lined up on the counter.

"Toby!" Good Boy says, before retrieving the bottles and tossing them into a bag. Toby sniffs the bag hopefully; kitchen scraps are his favorite, but the bathroom occasionally produces a cardboard roll or soggy tissue he can rip to shreds. Today, though, there's nothing but half-filled pill bottles, which taste bad and don't crumble in his teeth. Good Boy's hands tremble as he walks to the alley and empties the bag into the trash.

Afterwards, Good Boy can't make up his mind which room to stay in, so they crisscross the house. In the laundry room, Toby finds an old rawhide, which he swaps for the tennis ball under the desk in the den. He laps Good Boy in the living room and, when the doorbell rings, leaps against the window before Good Boy takes a single step. Outside, Mom does the knocking while Dog-Girl glowers from the porch steps, arms crossed. Good Boy puts a leg out before opening the door.

"I'm sorry to come so early," Mom says quickly. "Chloe is headed to school but wanted to . . ."

Dog-Girl keeps her back to them, even when Mom takes her arm. There's a pink swirl carved into the back of her hair and, even from inside, Toby smells new dirt beneath her fingernails.

"So I guess I was rude the other night," Dog-Girl says without turning around. She stares up at the clouds as if she wishes she were a hundred feet tall too.

"And you're sorry," Mom prompts.

Dog-Girl shrugs. "Sure."

Good Boy shakes his head. "Don't give it a second thought," he says, and Dog-Girl finally turns to face him.

"I won't."

"Chloe!" Mom's voice makes Toby flinch, but Dog-Girl merely steps off the porch.

"Bus is coming."

She disappears down the street as Mom tucks a stray curl behind her ear. "Well," she says, "I'd like to say she was sincere . . ."

"Really, it's totally fine. I had a great time."

Mom exhales slowly, perfuming the porch with the scent of coffee and cream.

"Listen," she says, "about the other night . . . " Once she starts talking, Toby finds an opening under Good Boy's knee and squeezes through. Mom barely even flinches when he circles her and licks her ankles.

" . . . especially hard on her," she continues. "Then there's Max . . . thinks I don't know . . . even with counseling . . . just fallen to pieces."

Toby's tail wags at the way Mom's voice starts and stops, but he prefers the silence that comes after, when he hears her racing heartbeat and the opening and closing of Good Boy's fist. The man never takes his gaze from Mom's face, even when Toby slinks down the porch steps and chews on a juniper branch.

"Not bad," Good Boy says at last, "but I think I can top it."

He runs a hand over the back of his neck, failing to notice the cracking of the juniper branch as Toby tugs to break it free.

" . . . started with a few leftover pain pills," he says. "After Anna died I couldn't . . . Vicodin. Oxycontin . . . pretty soon you have to fake . . . then a few weeks ago I OD'd."

The branch snaps with a satisfying pop and Toby chooses a sunny spot in the grass to lie down and chew it up.

"Jesus," Mom says. "You win."

Good Boy laughs and, a moment later, Mom joins him.

"Are you okay now?" Mom asks.

Good Boy shrugs. "What's okay? I just threw out . . . try to do one thing better than the day before. Just one."

Toby rolls onto his back with the stick in his mouth, listening as their voices quicken, the moment when a smile bleeds into their words. The two of them finally notice him in the yard, the shredded remains of needle-like leaves scattered around him.

"At least you have Toby," Mom says.

Good Boy throws back his head and laughs.

The first day that LOVE doesn't come, Toby lasts until the afternoon before relieving himself in the den. He despises the smell of his urine inside the house. The stench penetrates every corner, but when Good Boy comes home to find him hiding in the bedroom closet, the man doesn't even search for the stain. Instead, he touches Toby's nose and dangles the hedgehog above him, but Toby doesn't get up until Good Boy opens the back door. Once outside, Toby sprints around the yard, completing a dozen laps before he can no longer smell himself. Then he collapses onto the lawn and eats grass.

"Toby, no!" Good Boy says.

Toby looks up briefly, then continues to eat. Later, he will vomit it all and feel brand new.

The second day that LOVE doesn't come, the urine stain grows rancid, and Toby doesn't sleep. He sits by the living room window, leaping at the sight of LOVE's car when it passes, then lowering his tail when the sedan doesn't stop. After wandering the house, he breaks into the pantry and stands on his back legs to dislodge the salted crackers from the top shelf. But once he tears open the box, he has no appetite. It's almost a relief when he returns to the window to find the ginger cat cleaning her paws in the yard.

When he scratches at the glass, she merely flicks her tail and steps into a patch of sunlight. Even his barking doesn't faze her; she turns her yellow gaze on him then pads lazily into the neighbor's herb garden, rubbing herself against a clump of mint. If LOVE were here, Toby would race out the front door and corner the interloper in two seconds flat. But all he sees down the street is a stray dog sipping water out of the neighbor's birdbath. Toby recognizes the barrel chest and sand-colored fur at once, but the ginger cat never flinches as Sunshine walks past. When the big dog disappears around the corner, the ginger cat slinks after him. Toby barks until he's hoarse, watching the last place he saw them until the streetlights come on.

On the third day that LOVE doesn't come, Toby vomits. There is no grass in it; just orange, bitter bile that burns the back of his throat. He throws up once in the kitchen and twice more on Good Boy's bed. Afterwards, he curls up as small as he can on the living room couch. By the time Good Boy comes home, the smell in the house is oppressive.

"What the hell?" Good Boy says. "Toby?"

Toby buries his nose beneath the sofa cushion as Good Boy cleans the vomit. The man finally hunts down the urine stain as well and coats it with a layer of bleach. After he's scoured each room, Good Boy approaches the couch slowly, and Toby makes no attempt to escape. After a beating, he'll have the chance to be good again. Perhaps get through a whole day without disappointing a soul.

But Good Boy doesn't hit him. He sits on the edge of the sofa and bends over Toby like a blanket, covering him from head to toe. Then he wraps his arms around Toby's aching stomach and holds him gently until he stops shaking.

"That's a good boy," he says.

The heat builds inside Toby's body until he's almost drowsy, then he tentatively licks Good Boy's cheek. The man reaches into his pocket and takes out his phone. He holds it to his ear and Toby wags his tail when he finally hears LOVE's voice.

" . . . here, but leave me a message!"

Good Boy closes his eyes. "Sylvia, I can't believe you'd . . . keys back . . . please don't come . . . "

He puts the phone back in his pocket and picks up Toby's harness and leash. Toby drops his head over the edge of the cushion, his stomach still tied in knots.

"Don't be ridiculous," Good Boy says.

The man walks to the front door and opens it wide. Toby's nostrils flare at the blast of fresh odors; he can hardly believe that Good Boy's leg isn't barring the door.

"I'm going," Good Boy says, stepping out onto the porch.

At the sight of Good Boy leaving him, Toby flings himself toward the door. Good Boy blocks him to clip the harness around his chest, which is more than enough time for Toby to determine that every smell on the street is brand new. Sunshine and the ginger cat's trail leads east. A hawk made a kill two houses over. On the sidewalk is a steaming pile of coyote scat.

"Don't eat that!" Good Boy says.

Toby wags his tail as a jogger breaks stride to pet him. The man's arms taste as salty as seawater, and Toby didn't even have to lunge to get a good lick! Bad days not only end, they matter as little as yesterday's scents. As the jogger trots off, the charcoal grill Toby smelled last week gives way to chimney smoke, wilting tomato vines spout the distinct fragrance of mold. Then Good Boy turns the corner and he smells what should be LOVE, except that the bubblegum scent has been replaced with blood.

Toby tramples the weeds in front of the dark man's house, sniffing out LOVE's rubber shoe soles, pressing his nose into a patch of clover speckled with saliva and spilt beer.

"Come on," Good Boy says, trying to tug him down the sidewalk while Toby lowers his chest to reach the house. Music shakes the windows —not deep and rhythmic like the voices in Sherlock's headphones, but jarring and shrill. Someone screams, and the moment Toby realizes it's LOVE he charges, yanking the leash right out of Good Boy's hands. His teeth are bared before he reaches the porch steps. He will fight even Good Boy to get inside, but instead the man pushes past him and shoves open the door.

The room is a blur of smoke and shadow; the only clear thing is the dark man on the floor atop LOVE. Her hands are in fists against his bare chest, his legs, covered in coarse, dark hairs, straddling her hips. Toby can't smell LOVE at all beneath the stench of sweat and semen. But when she lifts a hand toward him, he leaps.

The dark man grunts as Toby hits him square in the shoulder and knocks him to the floor. For a moment, the man tries to wrestle, but Toby quickly stills him with teeth to his throat. Everything beyond the frantic pulse in the dark man's neck is a blur of crying and nonsense. It takes a few minutes for Toby to even hear the dark man's pleas. "Get him off! Get him . . ."

Foam drips from the corners of Toby's mouth onto the dark man's neck. He hasn't broken the skin, but the stink of blood fills the room from the cuts on LOVE's lips and cheek. Good Boy drapes a shirt around her shoulders and talks into his phone while the dark man lies whimpering. Tears run from his eyes to his ears as Toby scrapes his teeth across his throat.

"Can I move?" the dark man whispers.

"I wouldn't," Good Boy says.

The room comes slowly into focus—broken bottles, an overturned chair, burn marks in the carpet and two on LOVE's arm. Toby's growl deepens. By the time he hears the sirens, it's the dark man's urine that soils the floor.

"I'm s-so sorry," LOVE says.

Good Boy takes her shoulders in his hands. "You did nothing wrong. I wish I'd . . ."

The rest is lost as strange men rush into the room. Toby growls at them too until Good Boy gets a hand on his harness and the strangers drag the dark man to his feet. There's a struggle while the dark man yells, so no one notices when Sunshine creeps into the room. The dog's legs have thickened and his rope is gone; every inch of him, Toby notes enviously, is covered in burrs and dust.

When Sunshine barks, everyone assumes it's Toby, which allows Sunshine to charge untouched across the room. Someone screams, Good Boy lets go of Toby's harness, and Sunshine takes a chunk out of the dark man's arm before one of the strange men jabs a blue light into his fur. The dog yelps and jumps back, but he is so wild now, not even lightning harms him much. By the time Toby leaps toward the fight, Sunshine has vanished into the night.

" . . . do something about these frickin' dogs!" the dark man shouts.

While one of the strangers tends the dark man's wound, the other approaches Toby with the taser.

"Whoa!" Good Boy says, but Toby is already running. The moment he makes it through the door, he picks up Sunshine's scent. The dog headed down a mile of alleyways, cut across a school playground, thencrept out past the abandoned orchard where rotted fruit splatters the ground. Toby catches up with him by the concrete wash, where Sunshine unconcernedly laps at the green, slimy water. Toby acknowledges the change in status by staying back until the brown dog has his fill. Even then, he drinks quickly while Sunshine raises his nose to the wind.

When they start out again, Sunshine leads, guiding them along the wash before turning north toward the hills. They slink through darkened streets, deadening their footsteps in dirt and puddles. By the time they reach the first pines, they're as silent and elusive as shadows. Even if someone was looking for them, no one would know they were there.

13

Toby bares his teeth in his nightmare, but when he opens his eyes, the ginger cat is still there. She showed up two nights earlier, walking boldly into their camp beneath a pair of towering ponderosas, and when Toby charged her, Sunshine rammed him backwards with one strike of his massive chest. Incredibly, the cat is now allowed to roam freely and nibble at the fish carcasses they scavenge from streams. She sleeps in a bed of Sunshine's fur, leaving Toby to curl up uncomfortably on rocks and thistle. Her stench is intolerable, but whenever he growls, Sunshine eyes him. Toby hasn't slept through the night since they reached the forest. He was brave when he was inside.

And when they walk, the ginger cat leads! She follows no pattern, heading four miles one way, backtracking seven, turning north, then east, then north again. Twice she finds old fire rings with scraps of charred meat, but mostly they dine on beetles and bitter chokecherries, then soothe their stomachs with grass. Toby wags his tail at the sound of backpackers, but the ginger cat steers them away. The higher they climb into the mountains, the dimmer the city lights below. But Toby never thinks of leaving. He stays with who he's given; he loves whoever is there, even cats.

And there are cool streams. Flocks of quail he can flush without being reprimanded. The times when Sunshine nips his ear playfully or races him, futilely, downhill. Good Boy comes to him when he dozes, carrying hedgehogs and supersized cans of food, and when he wakes Sunshine hasn't left him so all is well. But when the ginger cat suddenly changes direction and turns back toward town, he pricks up his ears. Here's the familiar valley of scrub oak, the slow-moving wash with its green coating of slime. Sunshine barely glances at the dog park, where a pack of giddy Labs think they're running wild. The big dog marks Toby's favorite lampposts, then stomps boldly across the ginger cat's front lawn. The man with the hose sits on his porch stoop, a cedar box clutched to his chest.

"Bella!" he says, fumbling for his cane. "Where have you been?"

Toby bounds past the ginger cat and knocks the old man backwards, licking his gray, crusty lips. Dodging the man's flailing arms, Toby snatches a yellowed handkerchief from his breast pocket, ignoring the gold ring that drops from its folds to the ground.

"Stop!" the man with the hose shouts. He recovers the ring and grabs his cane, jabbing it at Toby's chest. "Get out of here!"

Toby chews the perfumed handkerchief and sniffs the old man's wooden box. It smells familiar, more like the lilacs that grow along Good Boy's fence than cedar. He noses the lid, but the old man keeps poking him in the ribs with his cane, another excellent game. Toby shows off his dodging skills, then snatches the cane with one quick bite. His claws graze the man's arm as he flies down the driveway with his prize.

"Stop that! Stop!"

The cane scrapes the side of the boxy car in the driveway, then slams into tree trunks and fences as Toby races home. He gallops across lawns and through the ivy where the golden Lab pees, charging the last few steps to Good Boy's porch. There, he drops his trophy on the mat and scratches the door. When Good Boy appears, Toby throws his paws around the man's shoulders. Life is even better than dreams.

LOVE rushes out of the den, smelling like everything good again. Toby licks the glossy red burns on her arm.

"Where have you been, maníaco?"

Toby slaps his tail against the door, savoring their nonsense and the touch of their hands. He squirms between Good Boy's legs and waits until the last scratch of his ears before leaving to reconnoiter the house. There is his couch and the tasty table legs, the pink tennis ball he'd thought was lost forever, along with the bathtub ledge where Good Boy no longer sits. Now that the pee stain, along with its abhorrent odor, have been scrubbed from the den, there is a new bed in the corner, perfumed with LOVE's scents.

He sniffs her shoes and a drop of saliva on her pillow, then picks up one of her pink fleece socks and runs from the room.

"... on his eighth life at this point," Good Boy says.

Toby keeps the sock just out of their reach as he flies past them and leaps from sofa to chair. They might be yelling, but everything sounds like joy to him, even the pounding on the door. Good Boy opens it with a leg out, but Toby has spent the last few days hurdling fallen trees and boulders —one leap and he flies right through. He feels more shock than pain when the end of the cane collides with his throat. Gasping for air, he falls on his hip bone as the man with the hose looms over him.

"This dog attacked me," the old man bellows. "They're coming to put him down."

Last time Toby was in a cell, he looked to escape, but now all he wants is to be noticed. He shares a cage in the back with an emaciated German Shepherd; the man who brings their food pours kibble through a slot in the door. They have no beds, a pair of terriers up in first class keep them awake with their yapping, and by morning the German Shepherd loses control of his bowels. Still, the woman who hoses down the concrete never sprays them. She has white hair and skin nearly as black as his fur, like she fell right out of the night sky. She calls the terrified Shepherd "Baby" and strokes the dog's neck until he stops shaking. She even slips a biscuit out of her pocket for Toby.

"And you, my giant friend," she says, letting Toby lick her fingers. "You have a visitor."

Toby whines when she leaves, but she winks and returns almost immediately with the man with the hose. The old man leans on his cane and keeps back from the cage, as if Toby could break through the reinforced chain link at any moment.

"So this is death row," he says.

The woman who cleaned the mess says nothing. She stays in the back row, crooning to the dogs who normally bark and bite so much, no other human will go near them. If dogs are made for people, then she is made for dogs. Toby swishes his tail when she reaches through the cell to scratch his ear, adding one more person to the ones he loves.

"You think I'm horrible," the man with the hose goes on.

The scent of the ginger cat radiates from the man's clothes. There are strands of her fur, and a few of Sunshine's, on his trousers.

The old man gestures at the German Shepherd. "Did he tear someone's liver out?"

He laughs, but he's trembling. Even with his cane, he can barely stand upright. Tears leak from the corners of his eyes, but when Toby pushes his snout through the chain link, the man whacks his cane against the cage. Half a dozen dogs howl.

"Sir," the woman made for dogs says.

The old man shakes his head. "Phyllis is gone and my Bella . . . deserve to walk out my own door and not be afraid."

After he leaves, the woman made for dogs opens the kennel door and steps into their cell. Toby presses as much of himself against her as possible; the German Shepherd lowers his head into her hands. When she speaks, Toby understands her perfectly.

"I'm going to miss you," she says.

The dream is a good one, so when they come to his cell to wake him, Toby keeps his eyes closed and doesn't let it go.   He can still see the ginger cat turning to stone, and Dog-Girl's garden of rusted spoons.   LOVE is there too, lying on a giant couch made of rawhide, but it's Good Boy that he's been waiting for.   Good Boy, who appears out of thin air looking like everything Toby has ever wanted.   And so Toby becomes exactly what is wanted too—the size of a terrier, fluffy, obedient and tame.

Then the scent of fresh cut grass and bubblegum swamps the room and, even in his dream, Toby barks for joy, too happy to be well-behaved. LOVE bends down to dance with him, until he realizes it's not dancing at all.   She has a hand around his chest and is pulling him to his feet.

And life, as it always does, gets better the moment he opens his eyes.

He is in his cell, but the door is open.   LOVE laughs and kisses his nose.   The woman made for dogs smiles, the German Shepherd throws back his head and howls.   The man with the hose stands on the other side of the chain link, his pants now covered with more of Sunshine's fur than the ginger cat's.   He doesn't whack his cane, but merely points it at Toby.

"You're lucky I'm so nice," he says.

Then Good Boy rushes in, and Toby's jubilation comes out like a cry.   He flies out of his cell and lands on the man's chest, licking his neck, his face, his ears, and listening to every word.

"We're going home now, Toby. Good boy."

14

Many years later . . .

Instead of the hated harness, Toby wears a yellow collar with a small metal tag too insignificant to chew to bits. Good Boy often leaves the front door wide open, but Toby never goes anywhere until he stretches and gets a good leg rub. Some days he'll fall right back to sleep until Good Boy nudges him.

"Come on, old man," Good Boy says.

Toby follows because it makes Good Boy happy, and because the pain in his legs and hips is no match for a stomachful of grass. All breeds of upstart dogs pee on his lawn now; a new generation of chipmunks chatter from trees he no longer tries to scale. And the ginger cat lives! Even after Toby and Good Boy moved to Mom's house, she found him, curling up beside him in the grass as if they were never anything but friends. Toby is cold and she is warm, so he doesn't bite her. Sometimes he even looks for her when she's gone. His black fur is streaked with white and he can't recall what real speed felt like, but he remembers how the cat used to sit where the woman on the fence once did, her long tail swishing while he and Sunshine raced on either side of the wall. There were enough gaps between the fence slats for Toby to know when he had the big dog beat, which was usually before the man with the hose came out and sprayed them both.

"Godforsaken idiot dogs," the man always said before rubbing Sunshine with a towel until he gleamed. This happened every day until the year of the freak snowstorm, when Sunshine didn't come outside anymore. Then one day a terrier appeared on the other side of the fence and there were no more races. Neither Toby nor the ginger cat even glanced in the terrier's direction when he yapped.

There is no more kibble. Toby has little appetite, but everything he eats now comes from a can! In addition to the pain in his hips, he also gets aches in his stomach and shooting pains from the lump that grows by his throat. He tries not to yelp when people pet him, but obviously he prefers Mom's gentle touch. Her house is better too, with more beds to commandeer when someone helps him up onto the mattress, along with a plush rug to lie on when he's alone. Not to mention the soft spot he's clawed out beneath the scarlet tree and the sunny patch near the garden he no longer bothers to excavate.

Aaaaaaaa is still there, less soft and smelling more like musk than candy, but he has a friend he calls Babe who squeals whenever Toby licks her face. Sherlock's old room sports a weight set and treadmill now, and when he visits he forgets his headphones, bringing LOVE and a curly-haired child instead. The little girl likes to climb on Toby's back and say, "Hiya!" but now that Toby can't bear her weight, LOVE holds the girl's hand and says, "Gentle, mi amor." Dog-Girl comes only once a year, and when she does she sits outside and rests her hand on Toby's head. Her hair is lighter, her skin darker, and she doesn't stay long. She has forests and rat buildings of her own.

He is never alone. Even when Aaaaaaaa jumps into Babe's car and Mom and Good Boy scratch his ears before driving off, the ginger cat always finds him. Even the shadow arrives every now and then. Like Dog-Girl, it stands apart, just a visitor now in someone else's home, but instead of darkness, it is light—bright enough that the ginger cat hisses at it until Sunshine arrives. The golden dog runs circles around them all, his tail emitting sparks the ginger cat bats away. They are all Sunshine, and though Toby often feels sleep overtaking him, he fights to keep his eyes wide open so he won't miss a moment.

Life is glorious!

About the author

Claire Dean, who also writes as Christy Yorke and Christy Cohen, is the author of 11 published novels, including Girlwood, Spirit Caller, and The Wishing Garden. She lives in Boise, Idaho with her husband, Robert, and Jenny, a Great Dane/Labrador/Jerk mix. The pseudonym Claire Dean is taken from the names of her two children, and only used for the books of her heart. The idea of writing a book from a dog's point of view was brewing for years, but the story really came together once Jenny, aka "the worst dog we ever had," came into the author's life. All of Claire Dean's novels have a dog running around in them somewhere, but Jenny wants to make it clear that she is the first star.

Made in the USA
Monee, IL
27 August 2020